Confidentially YOURS

Brooke's Not-So-Perfect Plan

1

ALSO BY JO WHITTEMORE

Confidentially Yours #2: Vanessa's Fashion Face-Off

JO WHITTEMORE

Confidentially

YOURS

Brooke's Not-So-Perfect Plan

1

HARPER

An Imprint of HarperCollinsPublishers

Library of Congress Control Number:
2015948302
ISBN 978-0-06-235893-6

Typography by Kate J. Engbring
15 16 17 18 19   OPM   10 9 8 7 6 5 4 3 2 1

First Edition

For Kristen Kittscher.
She knows why.

Contents

CHAPTER

1

The Three Musketeers

"Look, I'll show you how to juggle the soccer ball *one* last time," I told Vanessa. "I can't watch you hit yourself in the face again."

"To be fair, I thought we'd be using our hands," she said, rubbing her nose. "And juggling something softer . . . like puppies." A bright pink spot stood out against her skin. If *I'd* been smacked with a soccer ball that many times, my entire face would be as red as my hair.

I tightened my ponytail and took a few steps backward on the school's front lawn. "I'm going to bounce the ball from foot to foot to knee to chest"—I pointed to myself—"and then deflect it to you to hit with your head." I pointed to her. "Got it?"

Vanessa made a face. "Why did I agree to this?" she asked.

"You said you had first-day jitters," I reminded her, balancing the ball on the top of my head. "And the best way to get over them is by distracting your brain. Ready?"

"As I'll ever be," she said, dropping into a squat. Not so graceful for a girl in a wrap skirt, but my fashionista best friend never seemed to care what other people thought. "Come on, Brooke!" she urged me. "School's about to start."

At those words, my arms broke out in goose bumps. Vanessa's jitters had jumped to me . . . but who could blame either of us? This was our first day as middle schoolers!

I shivered with excitement and dropped the ball onto my foot. With the flick of an ankle, it bounced to the other foot, where I popped the ball up waist-high. From there I bounced it on my knee and then leaned back to catch it on my chest. I deflected the ball off me and straight to Vanessa.

Who caught it with her right eye.

"Owww!" She clapped a hand over the side of her face.

"Oh my gosh!" I ran to her. "Are you okay?"

Several kids getting off a bus stopped to stare.

"Theater auditions!" I called to them. "*Ow: The Musical.*"

Vanessa lowered her hand and blinked up at me. "How bad is it?"

"Well . . ." I winced. "Are eye patches in style by any chance?"

She stared at me for a moment and then burst out laughing.

One of the things I love about my best friend? Nothing keeps her down.

"I don't know how you do it, Brooke," she said, rubbing her face. "Soccer's hard . . . especially the ball."

"Awww." I hugged her. "Sorry. I guess I'm just used to it."

"Used to it" was putting it mildly. I've been playing since first grade, and last year I even joined a traveling team, the Berryville Strikers. We came really close to the state championship. This year, that title's ours!

"Maybe you should see the nurse before homeroom," I told Vanessa. "Your face is covered with splotches now."

"Not a problem," she said, reaching into her backpack. She pulled out a slick black case and snapped it open. It was full of eye shadows, blushes, and bronzers.

"I still can't believe your mom agreed to let you wear makeup," I remarked. "You must be the only twelve-year-old in eyeliner."

"I'm pretty sure she got sick of me stealing her stuff," Vanessa said with a grin.

Grabbing a thin makeup brush, she dabbed it in a few colors and swept it across the red spots on her skin. In a matter of seconds, her face was an even mocha tone.

"Amazing."

"I'm still gonna get some ice from the nurse, though," she said, studying her reflection. "I don't want to start middle school as a one-eyed freak."

"At least you'd be on the front page of the *Lincoln Log*," I teased her.

The *Lincoln Log* was our school newspaper . . . one that Vanessa; our other best friend, Heather Schwartz; and I would be working on in our Journalism elective class. We were hoping to get "the Three Musketeers"—our nickname from elementary school—as a byline.

"Don't you dare put me on the front page!"

Vanessa said, narrowing her eyes. She quickly shifted to a smile. "I'd rather be in the style section."

We walked under a giant stone arch with "Abraham Lincoln Middle School" carved into it and stopped just outside the front doors.

"This is it!" said Vanessa with a broad, toothy smile and a nervous bounce. "Sixth grade!"

I nodded and grinned back. "Big things are going to happen for us this year. I can feel it."

"Let the adventure . . . begin!" She pushed on the door.

It didn't budge.

"I think you have to pull," I said.

"Oh." Vanessa yanked on the door handle. "Let the adventure begin!" she repeated.

A rush of unfamiliar sounds, smells, and sights attacked my senses. I tried to find something or someone I recognized while Vanessa hooked her arm through mine.

"Everyone's so tall," she whispered, gazing up.

"Maybe we don't drink enough milk," I mumbled back. I opened my binder and pulled out a campus map, but Vanessa immediately slapped it out of my hand.

"Don't let them see that! They'll think we're tourists!"

I shot her a confused look. "Huh?"

She shook her head and picked up my map. "Sorry, it's something my mom says when we're in Chicago. Defensive reflex."

I found the nurse's office on the map, and Vanessa and I braved the crowd in the hallways, stopping just outside the nurse's door.

"Save me a seat in homeroom!" Vanessa called as I walked away.

"I probably don't have to!" I shouted back with a grin.

Any time a teacher sat us by last name, it was almost guaranteed that Brooke Jacobs would be sitting behind Vanessa Jackson. The only thing missing?

"Heather!" I called, spotting her outside the music hall. No surprise, considering she's in choir. Vanessa and I are always begging her to sing our favorite songs because her voice is amazing. Like, pop-star-meets-angel amazing.

Heather smiled and waved at me, then went back to her conversation with another dark-haired girl, Gabby Antonides.

I darted through the crowd to join them.

"Hey, guys!"

"Hey!" Heather's voice was soft but excited. "Can you believe we're finally here?"

"No more elementary school. No more pee puddles from the kindergarteners," I said.

Heather giggled. "Or first graders crying when the lights go out."

"Ha! You think it stops there?" asked Gabby. "My brother's still afraid of the dark."

Heather and I laughed.

Gabby's twin brother, Tim, was a giant and a jock. Not exactly the kind of guy you'd expect to need a nightlight.

"So how was your summer?" I asked Gabby.

She rolled her eyes. "Good and bad. I met this cute boy at camp—"

"Good!" I gave a thumbs-up.

"But I kind of lied and said I was the most popular girl in school."

"Bad." I gave a thumbs-down.

"And it turns out he lives in Berryville."

"Worse." I used the thumb to cut off my head.

"Oh, stop," said Heather, bumping me with her hip. "You're scaring Gabby." She took our friend's hands. "You guys don't even go to the same school, so it may never come up. But if it does, tell him the truth and apologize. Say that you were nervous and wanted to impress him."

Gabby's expression grew anxious. "You don't

think he'll hate me?"

"No," Heather said firmly. "There is too much nice about you to hate."

Gabby beamed and hugged her. "I should get going." She waved at us and then ran off.

"I'll never have your knack with people," I told Heather. "But you probably knew that after . . ." I repeated the head-slicing gesture.

She smiled, but held it back just enough to keep her teeth from showing.

Heather is pixie cute but really self-conscious about this teensy-tinesy gap between her front teeth. Vanessa and I have secretly made it our goal to get real smiles out of her all the time.

"First day of school!" I said, trying again.

All Heather did was squeal and grab my hands. "Where's Vanessa?" Heather stood on her tiptoes to peer over the crowd. "She should be with us for this!"

"She went to the nurse's office," I said. "Soccer

ball to the face. Many times."

Heather sighed and shook her head. "That girl needs to design herself a Bubble Wrap wardrobe."

The bell rang, and Heather and I faced each other with wide, excited eyes.

"It's time," I said. "The start of middle school!"

Heather squeezed my hands and squealed again. "Good luck! See you in Journalism!"

"Watch out for hungry eighth graders!" I told her, and darted off to find my homeroom.

Since each grade has its own hallway, it wasn't too hard to find. Plus, our homeroom teacher, Ms. Maxwell, had tacked a huge sign outside her door that said, "Welcome, F through J!"

She was standing in the classroom's entrance with an armful of packets, handing one to each student who entered.

"Good morning!" she said when I stepped closer. "Name?"

"Brooke Jacobs," I said.

"Welcome to Lincoln Middle School, Brooke!" She handed me a packet. "And here is your middle-school survival kit."

"What's inside?" I asked, feeling the weight of it.

"Just some tips about getting the most out of middle school, important dates and room numbers, and information about this year's clubs."

"Clubs? Awesome!" I glanced past her into the classroom. "Um . . . where do I sit?"

Ms. Maxwell held her arms open. "Anywhere you want!"

I staked out two desks in the corner and threw my bag on one of them for Vanessa. After saying a few hellos to the kids I knew, I opened my packet and pulled out the club sheet and a pen, poring over the list.

"Hey! Whatcha doing?" asked Vanessa. She slid into the desk behind me with a wet towel over half her face.

"I'm choosing clubs. What's this about?" I lifted the corner of the towel.

"I'm using a cold compress to reduce swelling," she said. "What clubs are you looking at?"

I handed her the page, and she whistled. "Dang, girl. You circled almost all of these! Art, athletics, band, cooking—"

"I'm hoping they'll let us make pizza."

Pizza is my favorite, pepperoni in particular, and should, in my opinion, be its own food group.

Vanessa kept reading all the way to the end. "Young Sherlocks?"

"I think I'm pretty good at solving mysteries," I said. "Remember that smell in my bedroom? Finally found the source."

She wrinkled her nose. "Well, I, for one, am sticking to whatever will further my fashion career." She frowned. "Which is absolutely nothing on this list."

"What about theater?" I asked. "You could help with costumes and makeup."

Her eyes lit up. "Ooh. Good point!"

I scanned the list. "And Model UN is probably going to want flags or outfits to represent the different countries. Like . . . those overalls and pointy hats for Germany."

"Um . . ." Vanessa wrinkled her forehead. "I'm pretty sure people wear suits for UN meetings."

"Really?" I raised my eyebrows. "I always pictured it like It's a Small World at Disney. How disappointing."

The rest of homeroom and my morning classes (math, PE, and English) went pretty much like elementary school, except with different teachers for each one. And, horror of horrors, homework on the very first day!

At the end of English, every kid in my class scrambled for the cafeteria and our first taste of freedom: lunch. All of sixth grade ate at the same time, while the upper classes ate in later shifts. Probably to spare the sixth graders from ending up in the trash cans.

I found my two best friends, and we claimed a table by the ice-cream cart.

"Middle school is *hard*, you guys," Heather said with a groan. She was in all advanced classes. "In science we're already prepping for our first lab."

"Oooh, what are you doing?" asked Vanessa. "Building a better human?"

Heather smiled at that. "I think we're smashing rocks."

"Too bad," said Vanessa. "Because my classes are seriously lacking in cute guys." She leaned closer. "I think it's so we'll pay more attention."

Heather giggled. "Could be. But I've seen some pretty cute ones in the older grades. Like Stefan Marshall?"

"And Abel Hart," I added. "But we're also

seriously lacking good PE teachers. I need to keep fit for soccer, and an hour of dodgeball isn't exercise!"

"Even though your soccer skills probably make you really good at it," said Heather with a smirk.

"Actually . . . the opposite," I said. "I'm so used to kicking anything that comes at me that I was out in the first two minutes."

Vanessa and Heather looked at each other and then burst out laughing.

"It's not funny!" I said, fighting back a smile.

"So what you really meant," said Vanessa, "was that *watching* an hour of dodgeball isn't exercise."

"Quiet, you!" I threw a grape at her. She deflected it, and it landed in Heather's pudding.

"Hey! I was going to eat that!"

"Like you can't sacrifice one thing on your tray?" I asked, eyeing Heather's lunch of tuna salad, chips, fruit, pasta, and cake. For a tiny girl, she can seriously chow down. I'm pretty sure she has extra stomachs, like a cow.

We chatted and ate until the bell rang. There was a massive groan from the entire lunchroom, followed by a scraping of chairs on linoleum.

"Journalism time!" I chirped. "*Lincoln Log*, here we come!"

"Save me a seat," said Heather. "I have to get rid of some chocolate pudding that somehow made its way onto my shirt." She narrowed her eyes at Vanessa.

"I'll help," she said with a sheepish grin.

I ventured to class alone, expecting the newsroom to be packed with students, shouting about deadlines and brainstorming ideas. But when I got there, I was only the third person to show.

In the front row a blond girl scribbled like mad in a notebook. Two rows behind her a guy sat with one long leg resting on top of the desk and the other in the aisle, tapping a beat with his foot.

The girl looked way too frantic to approach, but the guy was doodling a lion, the symbol for Chelsea Football Club, my favorite soccer team. I took it as a sign and sat beside him.

"Chelsea?" I asked.

He blinked at me. "No, I'm Gil."

I laughed. "I meant are you a fan of Chelsea Football Club?" I pointed to his drawing.

"Ohhh!" He laughed too. "No, it's Leo. You know . . . the zodiac sign? I do the horoscopes." Then he returned to his drawing and started bobbing his head to imaginary music.

I settled back in my seat and looked at the whiteboard while more students strolled in. Different sections and jobs at the paper had been written on the board with names beside them: *editor in chief, features, sports, entertainment, opinion* . . .

I frowned. All the positions were filled. What

was left for the Three Musketeers?

"Hey!" said Vanessa, dropping into the seat on my other side. "Why the long face?"

I pointed to the board. "What are we going to do? Everything's taken."

Heather took an empty seat in front of us. "Don't worry! We'll find something that's perfect for us. It's like my mom always says—"

"Hey! Sixth graders!"

All three of us snapped our heads around to look for the speaker. The blond girl who had been writing up a storm was now shaking her head with disapproval and pointing to the front of the classroom.

The teacher, Mrs. Higginbotham, waved at us. "Let's do a quick roll call before we get started, shall we?" She glanced at a clipboard and then up at the class. "Tim Antonides?"

"Oh, yay!" I said, looking around with everyone else.

On top of being Gabby's brother, Tim had played in a coed baseball league with me. He was fun to talk sports with, mainly because he didn't end each sentence by spitting, like the other guys.

But I didn't see Tim, and he didn't answer.

Mrs. Higginbotham called his name again before moving on. As students responded to the roll call, she jotted their names on a seating chart.

"Welcome to Journalism," she said when she was done taking attendance. "I see a lot of familiar faces and some new ones, but any input is always welcome. This class is an elective, but you'll still be graded based on your contribution to the newspaper. Our first issue will be what we call 'the short issue,' since the school year starts on a Wednesday and we don't have an entire week's worth of news yet. Nevertheless, I expect the sections to have their pieces in by Friday, and I expect quality material."

The blond girl raised her hand and stood to

face the class before Mrs. Higginbotham could say another word.

"Greetings, everyone," the girl said with a tight smile and curt nod. "My name is Mary Patrick Stephens, editor in chief of the *Lincoln Log*."

Her tone made it sound as if she were president of the United States.

"Since it's my final year with the paper, I want it to be a great one. This means brilliant stories and hard-hitting journalism." She pounded a fist into her hand. "Articles that would make Woodward and Bernstein proud!"

Vanessa leaned toward me. "What do woodwinds and Burt's Bees have to do with anything?"

I put my finger to my lips.

Mary Patrick spun toward Mrs. Higginbotham, blond hair fanning out around her shoulders. "You can count on this journalism team, Mrs. H. We will not let you down!"

Mrs. Higginbotham regarded her with wide

eyes. "Th-thank you, Mary Patrick. You can be seated."

"She's a little intense," Heather whispered over her shoulder.

I nodded, but deep down, I admired Mary Patrick's commitment to the paper. It was like me, with soccer. I'd practice as long and hard as it took to be the best.

Mrs. Higginbotham clapped her hands and looked at the rest of us. "As I said, the short issue is due Friday for release next Monday. I don't want you to worry about layout yet; I'm more concerned with content. Most of you know your jobs, but we have half a page that needs to be filled." She sighed. "Zack's still on probation for his article 'No Pants Day.'"

Several people giggled, but nobody volunteered to write for the half page. My hand shot up.

Mrs. Higginbotham pointed to me and

glanced at her seating chart. "Yes . . . Brooke, is it?"

Whoops. I'd been so excited for the space, I hadn't actually come up with anything. "Uh . . . we . . ."

I looked to Vanessa and Heather, who smiled encouragingly. I racked my brain frantically. What could we all talk about? Our interests were so different that we were always giving each other . . .

"Advice!" I blurted. "The Three Musketeers could do an advice column!"

Mrs. Higginbotham wrinkled her forehead. "The who?"

Several people giggled again.

I blushed and gestured at Vanessa and Heather. "I mean the three of us. I could give advice on fitness and sports"—the more I thought about it, the faster I spoke—"Vanessa could do beauty and fashion, and Heather's great with friendships and relationships."

"An advice column." Mrs. Higginbotham chewed the end of her marker.

Mary Patrick twisted in her seat to look from us to Mrs. Higginbotham. "That's not really hard-hitting news," she said. "Couldn't they do an exposé column, digging up dirt inside the school? Because I'm pretty sure there's actual dirt in the cafeteria mud pie."

"I think Brooke's idea is brilliant," said Gil, leaning over to high-five us. "The perfect balance to horoscopes. Advice from the stars . . . and advice from the students."

Mrs. Higginbotham smiled. "Advice column it is." She turned toward the whiteboard. "Brooke and . . . ?"

I repeated the other names while she jotted them in squeaky marker. The moment her back was turned, Tim Antonides sneaked into the classroom, gym bag over one shoulder.

"You must be Tim," said Mrs. Higginbotham, still scribbling away. "And you must be late."

He froze midcreep. "Sorry. I got lost."

"That's fine," she said, turning around. "Because you're just in time for your new assignment. You'll be working as an advice columnist with Brooke, Vanessa, and Heather."

"What?" Tim and I both said at the same time.

So much for the Three Musketeers.

"It's perfect," said Mrs. Higginbotham. "Advice from both the female and male points of view!"

"But . . . can't I do sports?" asked Tim.

"My turf, bro," said a ridiculously cute guy sitting next to Mary Patrick.

Heather let out a high-pitched giggle.

He had to be Stefan.

His hair was slightly sun-bleached, and his eyes matched the blue in the T-shirt he was wearing. The words *Swim for Sport* were scrawled across the front, and he pointed at the word *Sport*, as if to prove his point.

Tim snorted. "Swimming isn't a sport. It's just . . . not drowning."

Mrs. Higginbotham cleared her throat. "Nevertheless, Stefan *is* our sportswriter and lead photographer. I'd really appreciate it if you'd handle advice with . . . the Three Musketeers." She winked at me, and people snickered again.

Tim sighed but nodded. "Fine." He turned to Vanessa, Heather, and me. "Guess I'm your d'Artagnan."

The three of us exchanged mystified looks.

"Who?"

He opened his arms. "You know . . . the fourth Musketeer?"

Vanessa laughed. "Nooo, I'm pretty sure the candy bar wrapper says three."

Tim rolled his eyes. "I meant from the book? Don't you guys read?"

"About soccer," I said.

"About fashion," said Vanessa.

"About cute guys and doomed relationships," said Heather.

"This is gonna be great," muttered Tim.

Other kids in the room were already breaking into their sections to talk, so I motioned for Tim to scoot closer, and we all shifted our desks together.

"Three things," I said to him, Heather, and Vanessa. "One, we need a team leader. If everyone is okay with it, I nominate myself."

The others shrugged and nodded.

"Great! Two, how do we let people know about our column, *and* three, how do we decide whose turn it is to give advice?"

"How about we all answer a question every week?" asked Vanessa. "We can keep the answers short and sweet."

"And we could hand out flyers during classes to let people know about the column," said Heather. "And maybe ask for more questions at the end of each issue."

"With a drop-off box outside this room for kids to turn in their questions," added Tim.

"Great ideas!" Mrs. H strolled up to our table. "I like where this team is headed. Since the advice column is a new feature, we won't have letters yet to post in the short issue, but we can introduce the four of you, and I'd also like you to come up with a flyer to encourage kids to write in. Do you have a section leader?"

I raised my hand, and she pointed at me.

"I'll be emailing all the section leads with any important updates, so I'll need your school-assigned email address."

While I wrote it down, the others brainstormed what to put on the flyer.

"Keep up the good work!" Mrs. H said once I gave her my info.

Vanessa pulled out her sketch pencils and designed a cute, catchy ad that we handed to

Mrs. H. She scanned it into her computer and photocopied enough for us to wedge in the door of every locker. She even let us leave class to do it before the halls were too crowded.

Journalism was by far the best class of the day. By the final bell, I felt like I'd shrunk a foot from the weight of the books I was hauling to Mom's car.

"Hey, honey!" she greeted me. "How was your first official day as a middle schooler?"

"Fun!" I filled her in while I munched on the trail mix she'd brought me. "And tomorrow during homeroom, we're having a club tour in the gym where we get to sign up for extracurriculars. I might join a few!"

"Wow," she said. "Sounds like you've got a lot going on."

"I know, I love it!" I beamed. "Middle school is awesome. But not"—I held up a finger—

"as awesome as soccer."

"I'm sure Coach Bly will be happy to hear it," she said, pulling to the curb by the soccer field.

After six hours stuck in school, I bounded across the grass and into the women's side of the locker room. There are about twenty of us on my U12 team for girls under twelve years old, and most of them were already in the room, changing into training gear. I greeted them and listened in on the conversation about our practice schedule while I switched clothes.

"I'm just saying, we're already coming here four times a week," a girl named Lacey contin- ued, waving a piece of paper. "Why do we have to practice on our own too?"

"Practice makes perfect," I said with a smile.

"Ugh." She crumpled up her paper and threw it at me. I caught it in midair.

"Hands down, touch the ground!" the other

girls shouted, and laughed.

It's something our coach yells whenever we accidentally reach for the ball while it's in play, since only the keeper can do that. Whoever breaks the rule has to drop and do push-ups.

I humored them with one push-up before uncrumpling Lacey's paper ball and looking at the schedule. Despite what I'd just said, I had to admit it was a little much. After this week, Coach had us down for two-hour practices every Monday, Tuesday, Thursday, and Friday, with scrimmages on Saturdays and an extra requirement of two hours of drills divided over our days off.

"This isn't so bad," I said, adding what I hoped was a reassuring smile. "If we want to win state this year, we've got to do what it takes, right?"

A couple girls nodded, and others murmured their agreement.

"Besides, Coach wouldn't give us anything he

didn't think we could handle," I said. "And if he sees this schedule isn't working for us, I'm sure he'll change it."

Lacey rolled her eyes and took back the page. "I suppose you have a point."

"Of course I do," I said. "Now, let's go out and tear up some turf!"

"Yeah!" several girls cheered, and followed me outside.

I sprinted across the grassy pitch, doing cartwheels and flips while breathing in the scent of earth dug up by my cleats.

Coach Bly had us practice shielding and feinting (guarding the ball and faking moves), followed by three-on-three matches with another set of strikers, girls whose main job it was to handle the ball and shoot goals. My partners and I stayed on ball most of the time, *and* I netted a goal.

In the car after practice, Mom and I talked

about how it went, even conferencing in Dad over the car's speakerphone. Mom has her own accounting practice and works from home, but Dad works for an ad agency in Chicago. He works late a lot, but he always wants to know what I'm up to and sets aside Sunday as Family Day.

"A goal? That's fantastic!" he said. "You're center forward again, right?"

"Of course!" I said with a smile.

My position requires making a lot of goals, but it also means I have to be really good at shooting, dribbling, and keeping the ball close.

"Well, good job, kitten. I'll see you and Mom in a couple hours."

"Bye, honey," Mom told him.

"We'll try and save some pizza for you!" I said.

Dad chuckled. "Love you both."

The evening went by in a blur of homework, dinner, playing with my cat Hammie, bathtime, catching up with Dad, and then bed.

The next morning, Vanessa tottered over to me in a pair of heel-less black boots that looked as if they were on backward.

"You're not gonna believe this!" she chirped.

"You haven't fallen once in those things?" I guessed.

She made a face. "I've actually fallen five times, but they're cute, right?" She lifted one for my inspection and almost toppled over. "They're called 'anti-gravity shoes.'" She held up a hand. "Don't comment on how accurate the name is."

"I would never," I said with a smile. "So what am I not gonna believe?"

She handed me a piece of paper folded and fastened shut with a heart-shaped sticker. "Someone left a note for you in the advice box. You have a secret admirer!"

"What?" I took the paper from her. The sticker lifted easily, and I gave Vanessa a look.

"You already read it."

She shrugged and laughed weakly. "I thought it might be an advice request . . . or an important note from the principal."

"Sealed with a heart sticker?" I unfolded it and read aloud. "'Hey. I think you're okay to look at.'" I lowered the note. "Well, my search for love is over, V. Start designing my wedding dress."

Vanessa rolled her eyes. "It's sweet. And some guys aren't great at expressing their feelings."

When Heather joined us and read the note, she agreed.

"He could've said nothing," she pointed out. "But he made an effort."

"To tell me I'm okay to look at," I said. But I smiled a little and tucked the note in the side of my backpack. "The bell's about to ring. Let's head to the gym for the club tour."

I hooked my arm through Vanessa's as she

teetered in her backward heels. "Ready, Lady Gaga?"

She turned to Heather. "Will you grab my other arm? It helps to have extra support when I fall."

"Or you could not wear those shoes," I said.

Vanessa shook her head. "Now that I'm officially providing fashion advice, I have to look the part. Even if it kills me."

"That's what we're afraid of, sweetie," said Heather. But she grabbed Vanessa's other arm anyway.

The gym had been set up with row after row of tables, with banners and poster boards for every club. There were already other sixth graders wandering among the rows, talking to faculty sponsors or eighth-grade reps.

"Go nuts!" Ms. Maxwell told us, gesturing to the open floor.

While everyone else scattered like ants

running from a magnifying glass, I pulled out the list of clubs I'd circled and walked to the station of the first one.

"So . . . what are we painting in art class?" I asked the girl behind the table.

"Painting?" She raised a pierced eyebrow at me. "This isn't kindergarten; we don't *paint*. We transfer oils to canvas using our *souls* as brushes." She held a hand over her heart.

"Sounds messy," I said. "Also sounds like painting."

"Well, it's not," she said with a scowl.

I moved on to athletics.

"Yeaaah, they made a typo in the system," the guy said. "It's supposed to be Mathletics."

No, thank you.

It went from bad to worse: Band was only looking for someone to play the triangle, the cooking club had *no* plans to make pizza, the debate coach just argued with me. . . .

I traveled from table to table until I bumped into Heather at Model UN. She waved a tiny colored flag when she saw me.

"I just signed up to be Ireland!"

"Dibs on your pot o' gold!" I said in my best Irish accent.

Heather smiled. "Did you sign up for anything?"

"Not yet, but I grabbed some flyers for stuff." I flapped the papers. "There's only one left on my list . . . Young Sherlocks."

"Don't bother," said a girl next to me. "They won't talk to you until you answer their riddles." She glowered in the general direction of their table, where a guy with jet-black hair and an emerald-colored T-shirt sat, staring blankly ahead.

"Abel Hart's running it?" My cheeks warmed as I remembered talking about how cute he was the day before.

"Can you believe it? He's only a seventh

grader!" said the girl.

I could believe it. Abel was technically supposed to be in my grade but had skipped a year because he wasn't being challenged enough. Unfortunately, he wasn't exactly humble about that fact. . . . One of the less-cute things about him.

"Won't talk, huh? I love a challenge." I waved good-bye to Heather and made my way to the Young Sherlocks' table. "Hi!" I greeted Abel. "Could you tell me about your club?"

He lifted his head to look up at me, eyes as green as his shirt, but instead of answering, he slid an envelope across the table.

"What's this?" I asked. "An explanation for why you can't speak?"

I flipped it over and saw that it was sealed with wax and stamped with a tiny bird. I opened it and read:

A girl is missing from her classroom. Someone

has left an orange peel on her notebook. What now? Email sacd@youngsherlocks.com by next Friday.

"What now?" I repeated. "I assume she's been kidnapped."

Abel didn't say a word.

"I'm right, right? So tell me about the club. When do you meet? What do you do?"

He cocked an eyebrow.

I decided to change tack. "What, you thought your easy riddle was too hard to solve? I figured out what happened to the missing girl, so you owe me answers."

Just like I thought, Abel's ego couldn't take it. "You didn't solve it!" he said. "I didn't ask what happened to her. I asked what happens next."

"Next, I'd call the police," I said.

Abel pressed his lips together and went silent again.

I considered having a staring contest with him, but the bell rang.

"You're an excellent conversationalist," I told him. "And I look forward to future get-togethers."

The annoying thing? His club was the only one I was interested in.

But I had Journalism to cheer me up that afternoon, with super-awesome news.

Vanessa, Heather, and I all went to the advice box together and peered inside, squealing at what we saw.

There were at least twenty slips of folded paper waiting for us. The students of Abraham Lincoln Middle School wanted our advice!

I reached for the questions, and we ducked into the Journalism room, gathering in our group's corner. I opened one of the folded slips and read aloud.

"'Dear Lincoln's Letters.'" I smiled. "I really

do love that name."

When we'd created the flyer, the four of us had saved the title of our column for last. Several ideas were bounced around, like "Honest Abe" and "Lincoln Logicals."

Finally, Tim had said, "What about 'Lincoln's Letters'? Abe Lincoln was pretty famous for all the letters he wrote to people. Even the ones he never sent."

Judging by the number of advice requests we'd already received, we might actually end up writing as many letters as Lincoln.

"Ooh. I think this question will be the first I answer," said Heather. She'd plucked one out of the pile. "A kid who's shy when her friends aren't around. I can totally relate."

"None of these really stand out to me," I said, shuffling through them. "Especially not the one asking how to rob a bank without getting caught."

Vanessa took that slip and crumpled it up.

"We're bound to get prank ones. And today's only the first day. We'll get more."

"You're right. Let's get these sorted," I said.

We split the advice requests into five piles, one for each of us columnists and one for pranks and random questions that didn't fit our categories.

"What middle schooler actually worries about playing the stock market?" I asked, tossing a paper in the fifth pile.

Vanessa read her questions. "There are some seriously fashion-impaired people out there. It's going to be hard to choose."

"What's going to be hard to choose?" asked Tim, dropping his bag by his desk.

We showed him the requests, and even though he'd been less than thrilled about writing for the advice column, his eyes lit up at the pile of people wanting our help.

"This is awesome," he said, reaching into his

backpack and pulling out a bag of chocolate. "Oh, and Heather," he said, "my sister wanted me to tell you that she took your advice about that guy she met at camp. They have a date on Saturday."

Heather beamed. "Yay! My first satisfied customer."

We all laughed.

"AHEM?" Mary Patrick strolled past with her hands behind her back. "The newsroom is no place for frivolity," she said. "You should be—" She sniffed the air. "I smell chocolate."

"Peanut butter cup?" Tim held out a Reese's.

Mary Patrick grabbed it and tore open the foil.

"We should be . . . ?" I prompted her.

But Mary Patrick was popping the chocolate into her mouth and taking another piece that Tim offered. "Huh? Oh, nothing. Carry on," she said, and wandered away with her treasure.

Vanessa, Heather, and I all gawked at Tim, who grinned.

"I was talking to Stefan"— he leaned close—"trying to buddy up to him so he'll let me contribute to the sports page, and he told me peanut butter cups are Mary Patrick's weakness, so I figured . . . " He shrugged.

"That," I said, "is brilliant."

"What else did Stefan say?" asked Heather. I realized she was leaning in, chin rested on her palm, taking in every word with a dreamy expression.

"What else?" repeated Tim. "I guess . . . I guess he might have called me 'bro.'" He looked to me. "I'm not sure what . . ."

I shook my head. "It's fine." I waved my hand in front of Heather, who snapped out of her trance. "Hi!" I smiled at her. "Let's get to work. How about we write practice responses to some of these requests and share them?"

She blushed and nodded.

Vanessa already had a pen out and was

scribbling in her notebook.

Halfway through class, I used my very best teacher voice and said, "Pens down, students. Who wants to go first?"

Ever enthusiastic, Vanessa raised her hand.

"This is from Fur Real, and she says, 'Everyone tells me I shouldn't wear fur—'"

"She must be dating the stock-market kid," I said.

Heather put her finger to her lips, and Vanessa continued. "'Because it's cruel. What are my alternatives?'" She paused for emphasis. "And so I responded, 'Dear Fur Real, I'm glad to see your concern about our furry friends. Faux fur is just as soft and looks just as real for much less money. You'll be saving a fortune *and* lives.'"

Heather giggled. "Cute."

"'Love, Vanessa,'" she finished.

"Um," I said.

"No," Tim said, shaking his head. "I'm not

telling a bunch of girls that I love them."

"So sign your advice differently," she said.

I shook *my* head. "We should have a common sign-off, something that pulls all our advice together."

"'Your friend'?" suggested Heather.

"Too personal," said Tim.

"'Best wishes'?" offered Vanessa.

"Makes us sound a hundred," I said.

"'Sincerely'?" Heather tried again.

I chewed my lip. "These are all anonymous entries, right? So people know we're keeping their identities a secret?"

"Yeah," said Tim.

"Then how about 'Confidentially yours'?" I asked.

Nobody could argue with that.

"Okay, who's going next?" I asked.

Tim waved and picked up a slip of paper. "'Dear Lincoln's Letters, I'm an attractive guy. . . .'" He arched an eyebrow and flashed a toothy smile. We laughed.

"Are you sure you didn't turn that in?" Vanessa joked.

"'But,'" he continued, "'after gym I always smell like the monkey cage at the zoo. What should I do?'"

"Eat less bananas," I said.

Vanessa giggled, and Heather smiled. "What did he sign it as?"

Tim smirked and flipped the paper so we could see it. "He didn't use a fake name."

"Riley Cobb?" screeched Vanessa.

Heather clamped a hand over Vanessa's mouth, and Tim and I burst out laughing.

Riley was a sixth grader who was so babied by his mom that she insisted on driving behind the bus any time we took a field trip. It was pretty funny to imagine Riley's mom trying to wrangle his stink, but Heather was *not* amused.

"Guys, people are trusting us with their deepest, darkest—"

"Smelliest," I added.

"—secrets," she finished, shooting me a disapproving look. "If they provide their real names, it's up to us to alter them and to maintain their anonymity. Agreed?"

"Agreed," said Vanessa and I.

"I can't tease him just once?" asked Tim. "Maybe put a monkey poster on his locker?"

Heather narrowed her eyes at him, but the corner of her mouth twitched with a smile.

"Heather's right," I said. "We'll just pretend he signed it . . . Sir Stinks a Lot."

More laughter.

"Fine," said Tim. He cleared his throat. "'Dear Sir Stinks a Lot, to quote Shakespeare . . .'"

EHHHH!

We all jumped at the jarring sound.

"What the . . . ?" I turned and saw Mary

Patrick towering over us with a plastic buzzer in her hand.

She smiled indulgently. "Hi, team. I couldn't help overhearing the advice Tim was about to give. Can I offer some advice of my own?"

Tim sighed and lowered his paper. "Sure."

Mary Patrick placed a hand on her hip, assuming a know-it-all stance. "Shakespeare is *so* five hundred years ago. Literally. If you mention him to middle schoolers, you're going to lose readers," she said. "And I can't have that."

Tim stared at her. "This school needs some culture. You know what they were serving in the 'foreign flavors' line at the cafeteria yesterday? Nachos."

Mary Patrick smiled again. "Ethnic!"

Tim rolled his eyes, and I cleared my throat. "Look, I don't think his idea is a bad one. It'd be nice to let our personalities come through in our advice."

I glanced at Heather and Vanessa, who nodded their agreement.

"If Tim likes books, let him quote a Shakespeare novel," said Vanessa.

He held up a finger. "Actually, Shakespeare wrote plays and sonnets."

She gave him a withering look. "Do you want us on your side or don't you?"

Tim put his finger down and smiled up at Mary Patrick. "Shakespeare's novels are great!"

Heather leaned toward Mary Patrick. "You've done an amazing job with this paper, and the readers won't just give up on it. Plus, they'll really admire you for keeping such an open mind."

Mary Patrick glanced to one side before shifting her focus to the ceiling, as if praying for strength.

"Fine. But I want to see those response letters when you're done, and the second I start hearing negative feedback, you drop the dead poets." She pointed at Tim.

"Agreed," he said.

I nodded to her buzzer. "Where'd you get that?"

"My bad idea buzzer?" Mary Patrick held it out. "I pulled it from a Taboo game." She pressed the huge pink button.

EHHHHHHH! it screamed.

Vanessa made a tiny squeak, and Heather bumped her with an elbow. Tim studied the table and hid a smile.

"How very clever," I said, fighting back a laugh.

Mary Patrick didn't notice. "It's only temporary until the real one comes in."

I widened my eyes and smiled. "Can't wait. Now if you'll excuse us . . ." I turned my attention to Tim and gestured. "Continue with your letter of BO woe."

He, Vanessa, and Heather cracked up, though

I'm sure it had more to do with Mary Patrick, who was scurrying off to buzz someone else.

When Tim had composed himself, he straightened his paper with a flourish. "'Dear Sir Stinks a Lot, to quote Shakespeare, "Something is rotten in the state of Denmark." Or in this case, Berryville. And methinks it's coming from your armpit region.'"

This time I joined Vanessa's and Heather's laughter.

"'Now that you're getting older,'" Tim continued with a grin, "'deodorant and showers are a must after any serious sweating. Give those a try, and if they don't work, I hear the zoo has some vacancies. Confidentially yours, Tim Antonides.'"

We clapped, and he bowed. I read mine next, a question about the best warm-up exercises, and Heather went last, helping out the girl who was shy without her friends. As always, Heather's advice was thoughtful and kind.

She lowered her paper and frowned. "I wish this one wasn't anonymous so I could help this girl right now." She studied the pile of papers on the table. "I wish we could help all these people."

I pushed my chair back. "Maybe we can." I headed for the front of the room and told Mrs. H our problem.

"I can see your point," she said. "Let me think about this some more and discuss it with Mary Patrick."

Inwardly, I groaned. But for Mrs. H's benefit, I smiled and nodded. "Thanks."

The bell rang, and I hurried to catch up with Heather and Vanessa. Mary Patrick stopped me just as I reached the door.

"Oh, right! You wanted our practice response letters," I said, handing them to her. But she still didn't budge.

"What's wrong?" I asked. "Did your buzzer run out of batteries?"

"Why were you talking directly to Mrs. Higginbotham?" she countered, nostrils flaring. "*I'm* your editor. You should be going through *me*."

"Sorry," I said. "You're right."

She took a step back, apparently not used to hearing those words. Her nostrils calmed down, and she relaxed her shoulders.

"Look," she said, "I don't have anything against you personally, but I love this paper, and I can't let anything happen to it."

"Nothing will," I promised.

"I hope you're right," she said with a forced smile. "Because I'd hate to have to cut your column."

And with that lovely threat, she pushed past me and disappeared into the crowded hallway.

The Mesopotamian Shout

Heather and Vanessa managed to step out of Mary Patrick's way seconds before they were trampled.

"What was that about?" asked Vanessa, tottering in her anti-gravity shoes.

I shrugged. "She didn't like that I went over her head. I'm sure she'll get over it after a candy bar or two."

I didn't bother telling them about Mary Patrick's threat. For one thing, she didn't have the power, and for another, the advice column was already off to a great start. What was there to worry about?

Heather nudged my arm. "Ready for history?"

I groaned. Dredging up the past was bad enough, but we were talking about ancient civilizations . . . the Mesopotamians and Egyptians and Kush. The only fun part of that class was saying the word *Kush*.

When we got to class, the desks were arranged in squares of four and the teacher, Mr. Costas, was waiting at the door with a clipboard.

"What's going on?" I asked.

"Group project time!" he said with a smile.

"Already? But it's only the second day of school," I said.

"Why get your feet wet when you can dive right in? Ms. Jacobs, you are in Group One." He pointed to the farthest set of desks, where Tim's sister, Gabby, was already sitting.

I made my way through the groups, and

Heather started to follow.

"Ms. Schwartz?" Mr. Costas called. "You are in Group Four."

We glanced to where he was pointing, at some kids neither of us knew, and Heather gave me a panicked look.

"Want me to trade places with you?" I whispered.

Heather shook her head. "I wrote advice to Shy Violet that she should embrace new experiences, so that's what I'm going to do." She swallowed hard and approached the new kids. I watched her wave tentatively at them, and when one girl smiled back, I relaxed and sat beside Gabby.

"Hey!" she said. "First group project. Isn't this exciting?"

"I . . . guess? I'm not really big on history."

"Oh, I *love* it," Gabby gushed, crumpling the envelope she was holding in her enthusiasm. "I'm going to be an archaeologist someday. Like Mary Leakey."

I had no idea who that was, but if someone in my group actually enjoyed history, that could only be a good thing.

The other two members of our group joined us—a guy named Spencer and a girl named Ashley—and soon Mr. Costas was standing in front of the class, explaining our projects.

"You've each been given an envelope. Do not open it until I give the word. Within each envelope is a different civilization. You are to research yours and prepare a video about their lifestyle, due next Friday."

The room was suddenly abuzz with conversation.

"A video?" squeaked Gabby, clutching my arm. "This project sounds like fun!"

I gave her a thumbs-up and forced a smile.

This project sounded like work. A lot of it. In very little time.

"Mr. Costas?" I raised my hand. "Are we going to be able to get all this done during class?"

"I'll leave it to each group to schedule time to meet after school," he said.

We were then allowed to open our envelopes.

"Come on, Mesopotamia. Come on, Mesopotamia," Gabby chanted, ripping into the paper. "Yes!"

She held the paper up for us to share in her triumph.

Somewhere, crickets chirped.

"Okay, let's get started," I said. "First off, we need a team leader. If everyone's okay with it, I nominate myself."

By the end of class, we'd all chosen different lifestyle sectors to cover. Mine were food, money, medicine, sports, and leisure activities. I took a couple extra to make it easier on the others.

Heather wandered over when the bell rang. "Hey! What group did you guys get? We're Egypt."

"Mesopotamia," said Gabby. "It's gonna be a mess-o'-fun-time . . . e . . . ah." She looked from Heather to me. "I didn't pull that off, did I?"

I shook my head, laughing.

"That's okay. I'm an archaeologist, not a comedian. Off to the library I go!" Gabby hefted her book bag onto her shoulder and marched out of the classroom.

Heather and I grinned at each other.

"I think having a crush has given her more confidence," said Heather.

"What about you?" I asked. "How's your confidence with the new group?"

We made our way to the door.

"Good! Everyone's supernice," she said. "And one of the guys even has a dad who's in film production, so we're going to his house this weekend to start our video."

"This weekend?"

"Oh, don't worry," she said, putting a hand on my arm. "It won't interfere with Musketeer Movies."

Musketeer Movies was the name Vanessa, Heather, and I had come up with for our weekly girls' night. Almost every Saturday since we'd been friends, we go to Heather's for pizza and movies.

To be honest, with everything going on, I'd kind of forgotten.

"No, I meant . . . you're already filming your video? We're barely starting our research."

Heather grinned mischievously. "We're actually doing things a little different. Everyone's going to love it."

"Can't wait to see it," I said, although I didn't envy Heather spending her first weekend

working on school stuff. She needed an escape,
like I had with soccer.

I told Mom the same thing on the way to the
soccer field after school, and she shrugged.

"You girls are getting older now," she said.
"You're going to learn that fun can't always be
your top priority. Work comes first, and then
fun is the reward."

"But Dad works all the time," I said. "What's
his reward?"

Mom pulled into the parking lot. "Spending
time with us."

I snickered. "Poor Dad."

Mom tickled my side. "Go enjoy your reward!"

And I did. But it was exhausting. Coach had
us do wind sprints—running as fast as we possibly could—followed by passing drills and cone
maneuvers.

"Great practice!" said Coach as we were all

sweating and gasping on the sidelines. "And I've got some announcements for you. This year we're in need of a team captain—"

Instantly, my hand shot into the air, along with several other girls'. Coach Bly smiled and waved us all down.

"But this isn't a position assigned at random. It's earned. I'll be watching to determine who's worthy of the job, so if you're interested, sign up here." He handed a clipboard to the girl sitting closest to him.

"This year we also need to step up our game. I'll be providing each of you with an evaluation based on your position and years of play. The captaincy will give some of you incentive to try harder, but I've got something to give you *all* incentive." He held up several red envelopes. "Every week I'll be giving away a pair of tickets to watch the Chicago Fire play a home game."

Everyone cheered and whooped. The Chicago

Fire was our Major League Soccer team that had been topping the boards all year. And tickets to an MLS game weren't cheap.

I wanted those tickets. And that captaincy.

"The weekly winner will be determined by performance factors." He unrolled a poster board and explained the chart he'd created.

While he did that, I started mentally comparing myself to the best girls on the team. The toughest competition would come from Lacey Black. I glanced over at her at the exact same moment she glanced at me. We gave each other half smiles, but I knew what we were both thinking:

I'm going to crush you.

When Coach finished, he gestured to us. "I expect you all to play fair and play hard. Take tomorrow to recuperate and rest those muscles. On Saturday, we scrimmage!"

Instantly, our energy levels skyrocketed.

"Woo-hoo!" I crowed and chest-bumped

the girl closest to me.

When Mom showed up I galloped to the car.

"Good practice?" she asked with a smile.

"Scrimmage on Saturday!" I responded, slightly out of breath. "Oh, and Heather reminded me that we have Musketeer Movies that night."

Mom frowned. "Make sure you're leaving time for homework."

"It's the first week of school," I said. "I hardly have any."

She didn't look convinced. "You know there's going to be more work as the year progresses. Not to mention your training schedule."

"I'll manage," I said. "Can we have pizza for dinner?"

She laughed. "We can't have it two nights in a row!"

I batted my eyelashes at her. "Then can *I* have pizza for dinner?"

Mom rolled her eyes. "Let's go for something

healthier with more sustenance. You must be beat after that practice."

"I could play soccer all night," I informed her. "I've got loads of energy."

When we got to our driveway, I did cartwheels to the front door to prove my point.

"Impressive," said Mom. "Now cartwheel your way upstairs, change, and do your homework."

I paused just long enough to kick off my cleats and kiss Dad hello as he was coming in before taking the stairs two at a time.

As soon as I grabbed my math book and flopped down on my bed, though, a strange thing happened. I remembered how incredibly soft and comfortable my pillow was. I rested my head for just a second, with Hammie curled up beside me, before someone knocked on my bedroom door.

"Brooke, honey? Dinner!" said Dad.

"Wha?" I blinked and sat up, turning to look at my soccer ball clock.

An hour had passed.

And I was still in my sweaty, stinky soccer gear with an unopened math book lying beside me.

I scrambled to my feet, cat and soccer clothes flying in all directions as I changed into a T-shirt and shorts. A quick glance in my mirror revealed pillow creases across my cheek, and I pulled at my skin to try and smooth it out.

"Brooke?" It was Mom bellowing from downstairs.

I pulled open my bedroom door and walked down to the kitchen as casually as possible.

"HI!" I said in a cheery, fake wide-awake voice.

It must have been a little loud because both my parents jumped, and Dad almost dropped the spaghetti he was straining.

"Did you take a soccer ball to the ear?" he asked.

I blushed. "No, I am using the . . . uh . . . traditional Mesopotamian shout-greeting. We're studying them in history."

He nodded and pointed to the incriminating pillow creases on my face. "Are these Mesopotamian, too?"

"Uh . . . why, yes."

Mom shot me a warning look. "Brooke . . ."

"No, no," said Dad, putting the spaghetti pot on the counter. "I'd like to hear this."

"These lines"—I felt my cheek—"are a way of sending messages."

"On someone's . . . face?" said Dad with a raised eyebrow. "Why wouldn't they just use stone tablets?"

I chewed my lip. "You know how sometimes you can't find a pen? Sometimes they couldn't find tablets." I shrugged. "And . . . well . . . there were always plenty of faces to go around."

Mom coughed into the spoonful of tomato sauce she was tasting, but it sounded suspiciously like a laugh. Dad pressed his lips together and dropped spaghetti onto a plate.

"Thank you for that important history lesson, Brooke," he said, offering it to me. "You are so rich with information, I don't think you even need this week's allowance."

Busted.

I sighed and took the plate of spaghetti. "Fine. I fell asleep studying."

"Then you're definitely going to bed early," said Mom, scooping meatballs and sauce on top of my noodles. "No computer time after homework."

I grabbed a slice of garlic bread and trudged into the dining room. "Yes, ma'am."

Whether it was the carb load at dinner or the extra sleep, I woke up Friday morning completely recharged and invincible.

Homework? No problem. Soccer? No problem. History project? No problem. Newspaper? No problem.

And it was almost the weekend. How could it possibly get any better?

I checked our advice box, and mixed in with the requests was another folded note to me, sealed with a heart-shaped sticker. A smile sneaked across my face.

"All right, Secret Admirer, did you step up your game?" I asked, being careful not to damage the sticker as I opened the note.

You're different.

"'You're different'? What's that supposed to mean?" I squawked.

"That you're louder than other girls?" Tim appeared next to me and took the note. "What's this?"

"It's private." I snatched it back. "What are you doing here?"

"I wanted to see if we had any more advice requests. Do we?" He lifted the advice box's flap. "Score!"

Tim reached in and pulled out a scrunched handful. Then he sat against the wall and started reading them.

"What do you think 'You're different' means? Seriously," I said, sliding down next to him.

"It means he thinks you're different," said Tim, not looking up. "Guys aren't like girls. Our words don't mean five hundred different things. You can usually take what we say at face value."

"Oh, whatever." I put the note in my backpack. "What about when a guy says, 'It's not you, it's me'?"

He glanced up. "It's *not* you. It's me . . . not liking you."

I rolled my eyes. "Romantic."

Tim shrugged. "When a guy wants out, romantic doesn't matter. He just wants to escape with as little drama as possible." He held up a slip of paper. "Take this girl, for example. Her boyfriend broke up with her, and she wants to talk him into getting back together."

I thought for a moment. "Well, why did they break up?"

"Doesn't matter," said Tim. "She shouldn't be trying to convince him. He needs to decide to come back on his own."

I crossed my arms. "I don't like the rules of Guy World."

Tim laughed. "We don't like yours any better."

Heather and Vanessa walked up, smiling.

"Told you she'd be here," said Vanessa. "Any good questions?"

"I wouldn't know," I said. "Tim's hogging them all."

"Please. Help yourself." He held out the papers. "I've already dispensed a ton of wisdom this morning." He nodded toward me.

Heather and Vanessa gave me quizzical looks, and I explained the conversation.

"That's silly," said Vanessa.

Heather tilted her head. "I don't know. I think Tim has a point."

"About what?" I asked. "The note from my secret admirer or the girl who wants her boyfriend back?"

"Both," said Heather. "Your admirer thinks you're different from other girls—"

"In a good way," interjected Vanessa. "Or he wouldn't send a note."

Heather nodded. "But you can't read more into it than that. And the girl's ex-boyfriend needs to come back on his own. He needs to be the one to realize what he's missing."

Tim high-fived Heather. "And if he doesn't go

back, she'll know he wasn't the right one."

"Exactly." Heather chewed her lip. "Are you going to answer that one for the paper? Because I kind of want to now."

"I thought you were going to answer the one about the shy girl," I said.

"Yeah . . ." She scratched her head. "I guess I have to decide which is more important."

Luckily, she didn't have to.

That afternoon, Mrs. H greeted me at the door to the Journalism room. "Just the girl I wanted to see. I thought about your idea to help as many students as possible, and after talking it over with Mary Patrick, we've come to a solution."

"Really?" I looked to Mary Patrick, who was drawing red Xs all over someone's article.

"As you may or may not know, the *Lincoln Log* has a website where we post the articles, along with a few other interactive features. Your advice column will be on the website, where you can answer as many questions as you want!"

I gaped at her, openmouthed. "That's amazing! Thank you! The others are going to be so happy!"

Mrs. H beamed at me. "Make sure you include it in today's broadcast, okay?"

I smiled back, but through my teeth asked, "What?"

She chuckled and squeezed my shoulder. "The broadcast, silly!"

I continued to stare blankly at her.

"We're doing a live feed in a few minutes, introducing the newspaper team," said Mrs. H. "A Meet the Press event, if you will." She narrowed her eyes. "I emailed this info to the leads of all the sections."

My cheeks warmed. "I . . . haven't checked my email recently. Sorry, did you say 'live feed'?"

She nodded. "For the advice column, you'll

be introducing yourselves to the student body, and then I thought it'd be fun to show off your skills by each answering a question live on the air." She tilted her head to one side. "Will that be a problem?"

I let out a laugh that put my Mesopotamian shout-greeting to shame. "HA!"

Mrs. H. blinked and stumbled back a pace.

"Ooh, sorry," I said, grabbing her arm. "No, it won't be a problem."

I smiled at her reassuringly, swiveled on my heel, and speed-walked to the corner, where my friends were sitting.

"Problem! Problem!" I squealed.

Meet the Press

"Dude!" said Tim after I'd filled my team in. "I don't want the whole school to watch me!"

"Well, it's too late. Sorry," I said with a grimace. "Vanessa, can you take care of our hair and makeup? I want us to look as good as possible if we're going to make fools of ourselves."

"On it," she said, fishing a compact out of her backpack. "Tim?"

"No way!" He pushed his chair back and got to his feet. "I draw the line at makeup! One time I let Gabby play Pretty Princess with me, and I couldn't get the lipstick off for days."

Vanessa pressed her lips together. "I was just going to ask you to move so Heather could have your seat. But thanks for that fun tidbit."

"Oh." Tim shoved his hands into his pockets and blushed. "Brooke, can I talk to you for a second?"

"Sure, Princess." I took him by the arm, leading him away from Vanessa's and Heather's laughter. "What's up?"

He frowned. "I don't think I want to do this."

"You'll do fine. It'll just be in front of the camera a couple minutes, tops," I assured him.

Tim shook his head. "I mean I don't think I want to be an advice columnist. People are going to make fun of me. This is chick stuff."

I gripped his shoulders. "Tim. I'll be the first to admit that I wanted it to just be Heather, Vanessa, and me on the column."

"Nice pep talk," he said dryly.

I held up a hand. "That advice you gave me earlier? As much as I hated to hear it, it made a lot of sense. And you bring something to this column that we don't. Not just a guy's perspective, but also your sense of humor and style. We need you!"

"Can't we swap advice topics?" he asked. "I'll take sports and give you . . ." He paused.

"Choose your words carefully," I said.

He sighed. "Fine, it wouldn't work, but I still want to cover the sports beat!"

"And you may get that chance," I said, "but you have to prove that you deserve it. Dropping out of your column? Not the way to do it." I rolled my eyes. "Not to go all Mary Patrick on you, but it's highly unprofessional."

Tim snickered. "Yeah, I guess you have a point."

Vanessa ran up to us, clutching a handful of makeup cases and brushes. "Brooke, let's do this!

Mrs. H says we have five minutes!"

I took a deep breath and nodded. While she dabbed concealer on my face, I pointed to Tim. "Work with Heather and find a question for each of us to answer."

He nodded and hurried to the table. Out of the corner of my eye, I could see him and Heather rummaging through strips of paper.

No sooner had Vanessa stepped away from me and said "Done!" than Mrs. H clapped her hands.

"Folks," she said, "we're going live."

Twenty students had never been so quiet and so still for so long. The second the camera crew entered the room, we all sat up straight, like puppets on tightened strings. The guy holding the camera panned the room, and I watched the little red light as it passed over the advice team.

I could swear it watched us too.

Mrs. H smiled as the camera guy focused on

her, and she said a hearty hello to all students watching the broadcast. She gestured to Mary Patrick, who I thought would at least soften up for her readers.

But no, she slapped a ruler against her palm the entire time she talked about the discipline and commitment needed to run the paper and how happy—*whack!*—she hoped—*whack!*—we'd be—*whack!*—reading it.

"Is she hoping or threatening?" Vanessa mumbled out of the corner of her mouth.

"Shhh," I said, not taking my eyes off the camera. It had moved on to the front-page team. "Tim, hand me my question."

I felt him slip a piece of paper into my hand, crushing my fingers at the last second. "Ow! What gives?"

That's when I saw that sports was up, and Stefan was flashing a dimply, Instagram-worthy smile while he talked about what the students could expect to learn from his column.

"Nothing!" grumbled Tim. "Because his head is full of water, and his brain is pickled from chlorine!"

I turned to give Tim a warning look . . . and to reclaim my hand.

Next to me, I could hear Heather whisper-chant to herself.

"Red leather, yellow leather. Red leather, yellow leather."

When she realized I was watching, she blushed and shrugged.

"Speaking exercises," she whispered.

Vanessa was the only one of my team who didn't appear the least bit fazed by the cameras. I decided that I'd talk first, then Vanessa, then Heather, and finally Tim, if he could quit muttering curses at Stefan.

Mrs. H walked with the camera over to our table, talking the whole way.

"As you know, we're introducing a new feature to the *Lincoln Log* this year: an advice column. Every week, we'll be publishing a piece of advice in the categories of sports, fashion, relationships, and . . . guys." She faltered only for a second, but it was enough to deepen Tim's scowl. "The team would like to introduce themselves and offer you all a little bit of advice," said Mrs. H.

The camera panned to me, and I waved and flashed a smile.

"Hi, I'm Brooke Jacobs, head of the advice column, and I'll be answering questions about sports and fitness."

I opened the paper Tim gave me and said in a cheerful voice, "I like to eat boogers!"

The second the words left my mouth, I knew they were wrong. Also, the laughter from nearby classrooms was a pretty big clue.

Heather and Vanessa had their hands clapped

over their mouths. I whirled around to stare daggers at Tim, who was holding both his hands up in surrender.

"Sorry! That was a funny one I wanted to show you later!" he whispered. "I must have gotten them mixed up!"

He thrust a second piece of paper at me.

I took it and spun back around to face the camera.

"Ha, ha, ha!" I forced a laugh. "Wow, bad news for whoever sent that one I just read. Wish I could help"—I leaned in close to the camera—"but I, Brooke Jacobs, don't eat my boogers. Let's see what this student has to say!"

I managed to stumble through the question and give some decent advice, but I was grateful when the camera moved on to Vanessa.

Was grateful. For about five seconds.

A look of terror came over Vanessa's face, her eyes opening almost as wide as her mouth.

Stage fright.

"Vanessa?" I waved my hand in front of her face.

Tim popped up on her other side and spoke into the camera. "You'll have to forgive our fashionista. She's still in shock over Brooke's booger-eating confession."

Everyone snickered except me.

"I don't—"

"But you can tell by her outfit that Vanessa knows her stuff!" Tim clapped her on the shoulder. "She even did makeup for Brooke and Heather right before this broadcast! But not me. I have a natural glow." He batted his eyelashes, and the audience ate it up.

"Why don't we let Vanessa recover and move on to Heather?" Tim suggested.

"Oh no." I wanted to bury my face in my hands, but I was afraid people would think I was enjoying a nose snack. Instead, I steeled myself for whatever catastrophe Heather might bring. Utter silence like Vanessa? Maybe tears?

"Hello, Abraham Lincoln Middle School!" chirped Heather with a confident, friendly smile. One that showed *all* her teeth. "I'm Heather Schwartz, your relationship guru, and if it's broke, I can fix it!" She winked at the camera.

I watched her dish out the advice we'd discussed earlier for the girl who wanted her ex-boyfriend back, and I was amazed by how my shy wallflower friend had suddenly transformed into Miss Personality. When she was done, a couple people actually applauded, including Tim.

"Wise beyond her years," he said as the camera traveled to him. "And I'm Tim Antonides. I'm a Libra. I enjoy earwax sculptures, playing the piccolo—" He looked away from the camera and feigned surprise. "Oh, this isn't the time for that?"

More laughter from the classrooms.

He smiled. "Whoops. But I want to add, I am so very single, ladies."

I rolled my eyes.

"All joking aside," he said, "I'm here to provide the male perspective, so girls, if you need advice on dudes, or guys, if you need advice on *being* a dude, I'm your dude." He straightened out his strip of paper. "'Dear Lincoln's Letters, I gave this boy my number, and he never called me. What should I do?'" Tim stared directly into the camera. "Thank God he didn't, because clearly the boy can't afford a phone . . . or a backbone."

All the girls in our room clapped and cheered.

And then the segment was over.

Heaving the greatest sigh imaginable, I flopped the upper half of my body onto the desk.

"That was awesome!" said Tim.

"So much fun!" agreed Heather.

I swung my arms wildly, hoping to strike

at least one of them.

"Do you think I did okay?" asked Vanessa. "I know I was a little quiet, but . . ."

I twisted to look up at her. "Seriously?"

She frowned. "What? I get a little flustered in front of the camera."

"Ha! Understatement of the year."

Vanessa looked to Tim and Heather. "Was it that bad?"

Heather put a hand on her arm. "You may have frozen up a teensy bit."

"You were a Vanessicle," agreed Tim.

Vanessa's eyes bugged out of her head.

"That's a very good impersonation of your earlier self," I told her.

She bowed her head and sighed. "Did I do anything?"

"At one point you blew a spit bubble," said Tim. "But the camera was focused on Heather by then, so nobody saw. Probably."

Vanessa's lower lip trembled, and her eyes filled up with tears.

"Oh, but Tim talked you up!" said Heather, rubbing Vanessa's arm. "He mentioned your outfit and the *awesome* makeup job you did for me and Brooke!"

The tears spilled over just the same, and Vanessa's face crinkled up as she started crying.

I leaned over and hugged her. "Awww, it's not that bad. A lot of people get stage fright."

"But everyone thinks I'm this confident girl who's got it all together! And I just proved that I'm not!" she sobbed.

I squeezed tighter. "No. You proved that you're human. People can relate to that."

"She's right," said Heather. "And not everyone knows you, but the kids who do, know you've got style and are the best person to ask for fashion advice."

Tim held up his phone. "I've got proof. My

sister just asked if you'd do her makeup for her date this weekend."

Vanessa rubbed at her eyes and sniffled. "Really?"

"Yeah, apparently she's bad at putting on maracas." Tim frowned at his phone. "And bad at spelling *mascara*."

"Gabby doesn't need mascara," said Vanessa. "Her eyelashes already have a nice curl. All she really needs is some eyeliner. . . ."

Tim passed his phone to Vanessa, who started tapping away.

One crisis momentarily averted.

"How much do you think Boogergate is going to affect our column?" I asked Heather.

She smiled. "It won't. Even though everyone laughed, they know you were just reading what was on the paper. You'll get teased for a while, and then something new and even more embarrassing will happen to someone, and the attention will shift off you."

I regarded her solemnly. "Maybe you could actually eat your b—"

"No," she said. "I'm Jewish, and I'm pretty sure they aren't kosher."

We both cracked up.

Mrs. H wandered over to us, with Mary Patrick in tow.

"That was definitely an . . . interesting segment," Mrs. H said. "How is everyone?" She put a hand on Vanessa's shoulder.

"Embarrassed," said Vanessa, wiping the remainders of tears from her eyes. "But doing better, thanks to my team."

Mrs. H nodded. "Tim, I have to say I was very impressed by your quick thinking."

"Yes!" Heather and I applauded him.

He grinned and turned pink. "Hey, advice columnists have to be able to solve problems, right? I was just doing my job."

Mrs. H rested a hand on my shoulder next. "And don't worry about your little gaffe. I'm sure fewer people noticed than you realize."

Mary Patrick didn't say a single word; she just shot me a disgusted look.

I didn't bother hoping that Heather or Mrs. H might be right. I knew exactly how things would go down. Kids were going to smile or laugh when they saw me (which they did) and make jokes about having some boogers for me (which they did).

I glared at Tim, who had walked with me to deflect some of the damage.

"Sorry!" he said again. "But at least I was right. The note *was* funny."

"Hysterical," I said, opening my locker.

"Just give it a week. We'll all look back and laugh," he assured me. "How's soccer going?"

"Are you genuinely interested or just trying

to get me to stop hating you?"

"Both," he said.

"We've got a scrimmage tomorrow," I told him, "and I'm center forward, so it should be a lot of fun!"

Tim made a face. "Lucky. Our coach is having us take it slow this year. Since a lot of us are in middle school, he's worried we'll burn out. But honestly? I'm bored out of my mind."

"Which is why you want the sports page job," I said.

"Pretty much. You talk to Mary Patrick sometimes, right?"

I snorted. "Never about anything good." I pulled my history book out of my locker and closed it with an elbow. "Trust me, I'd hurt your chances more than I'd help them."

Tim sighed and leaned against the lockers.

"Just give it time," I said. "If you can keep up the awesome work you did during today's intro,

I'm sure Mrs. H will have you running the paper before too long."

He grinned. "I was pretty amazing, wasn't I?"

"I wouldn't be surprised if you had a line of girls waiting at your locker for dates," I said.

He raised his eyebrows. "Good point. I should get over there."

Tim waved and pushed his way through the crowd.

I dreaded going to history, but thankfully, Mr. Costas had decided to give us one research day in the library, where nobody was allowed to be disruptive.

And where nobody could torment me about my now infamous moment in the spotlight.

I wandered over to the reference area and started looking for ancient history books. Gabby joined me and said in a low voice, "Word on the street is that you know Jefferson Black."

Jefferson was my teammate Lacey's brother.

Occasionally, he came to watch her practice and then walk home with her.

"Yeah?" I whispered back. "So?"

Gabby just blushed.

"Ohhh," I said. "He's your date this weekend."

"Shhh!" She giggled and glanced over her shoulder. "Does he talk about me?"

I blinked at her. "He doesn't talk about anybody. He just sits in the grass and watches us play."

"Alone?" asked Gabby.

"Unless he has some imaginary friends," I said. "Then yes."

She squealed and hugged me. "Will you do me a favor? Will you mention my name and see how he reacts?"

This felt like impending disaster.

"Aren't you going on a date with him tomorrow night?" I asked. "You'll know soon enough."

"But that's *not* soon enough!"

I took a step back. "Oookay. If he's at the

scrimmage tomorrow, I'll mention your name and see if he giggles his head off."

Gabby frowned. "He's not a giggler. He's serious and tough."

Geez.

"Fine. I'll say your name and see if he does something manly. Now if you'll excuse me, I've got some research to do."

Gabby hugged me from behind. "Thank you, Brooke! I don't care if you *do* eat your boogers."

Several people close by snickered.

"I *don't* . . . Forget it." I grabbed some books and crawled under the librarian's desk to read. When the librarian sat down, she didn't even give me a second glance. I guess she's used to kids hiding from their problems down there.

I couldn't focus on Mesopotamia, so I pulled out the Young Sherlocks' letter and reread it. A girl just disappears, and there's an orange peel on her desk. Why?

Maybe she was allergic to oranges and some-one took her to the emergency room. Or maybe as she was peeling the orange, it came to life and ate *her*.

Or maybe the answer was already given in a Sherlock Holmes book!

I crawled out from under the desk and searched the library's database. We didn't have many books by Sir Arthur Conan Doyle, but they were all already checked out.

Clearly, I wasn't the only person who wanted to solve things the easy way.

I endured a few more booger-based jabs during science, and when the bell rang for the end of school, I sprinted toward the building's exit. At home, I gave my mom the brief school-was-fine answer for when school absolutely isn't fine, but you don't want to talk about it. Then I headed up to my room to read over advice questions sent into "Lincoln's Letters." I thought it might make me feel better to solve other people's problems, rather than fixate on my own.

I grabbed a handful and started trying to answer the first one, but my mind was swirling with the disastrous video session, the website, my history project, Tim not wanting to write for the column, Mary Patrick threatening to end the column, soccer, Musketeer Movies, my secret admirer, and all the homework I hadn't even started.

Instead of doing any of it, I did none of it. I simply stared into space and listened to Hammie purr while I stroked her. I was at least encouraged by the thought that tomorrow *had* to go better.

CHAPTER

5

Playing Games

Scrimmage Day!

I bounced out of bed and ran down to the laundry room, where Mom had hung my uniform to dry.

"Good morning!" she called as I flew past.

I changed on the spot, drop-kicking my pajamas into the washer.

"Gooooaaaaaaaal!" I roared, running into the kitchen with my arms above my head.

Mom gave me an amused smile. "I'm afraid to offer you some breakfast with the energy level you already have."

Nevertheless, she handed me a plate with eggs and bacon.

"I need carbs," I told her. "Lots of carbs." I pointed to a loaf of bread on the counter. "Can I have that?"

"You can have one slice," she said. "If you eat too much, you're going to feel sluggish and sick."

I sat down and sprinkled salt and pepper on my eggs. "Where's Dad?"

"He had to go into the office to finish a project," she said.

I wrinkled my nose. "It's ten a.m. on a Saturday. Isn't it against the law to make someone work so hard?"

Mom laughed. "It's his choice. He's wanted to get this project done for a while, but during the workweek, there are so many distractions."

I could definitely relate to that.

"But the good news is he'll be able to make it for the second half of your scrimmage."

"Woo-hoo!" I cheered.

While I was eating I checked my phone. Three missed messages, one from each of my advice column partners.

Heather: Good luck at the scrimmage! It's Musketeer Movies night!

Vanessa: Can't wait to see you and Heather tonight! Have fun at soccer!

Tim: My sister wanted me to remind you to talk to Jefferson.

I rolled my eyes at the last message and then responded to just Heather and Vanessa. Then I finished my orange juice and carried my plate to the sink.

"Do you think it's weird for a girl I know to ask me to ask another girl's brother what he thinks of her; not really ask, but just mention her name?" I asked Mom.

She blinked and shook her head. "Do what now?"

"Never mind. I'm playing Cupid, and I don't like it." I wandered back into the laundry room to get my shin guards.

"Well, just be careful!" Mom called after me. "You don't want to mess in other people's affairs if you don't have to."

"I write an advice column!" I told her. "Other people's business is *my* business."

I tugged on my shin guards and laced up my soccer cleats. She did have a point. Romance wasn't my area of expertise. I took my phone out of my shorts and called Heather.

"Hi!" she said. "How's soccer? Did you win?"

"We haven't even gotten to the field yet," I said with a grin. "Hey, listen. Gabby asked me to talk to Jefferson and bring up her name. How do I do that without being obvious?"

Heather sucked air through her teeth. "Eesh. I don't know. It's going to seem fishy."

"That's what *I* thought," I said. "But I

already promised Gabby."

"Okay, how about . . . maybe mention how great it is that Jefferson watches his sister practice and how it reminds you of your friend Tim and his sister—"

"Gabby!" I finished for Heather. "You . . . are a genius."

"They don't put me in advanced classes for nothing." I could hear the grin in Heather's voice. "Make sure you tell me how it goes. With Jefferson *and* soccer."

"Of course," I promised. "See you tonight!" I ended the call and *click-clack*ed down the hall in my cleats.

"Ready to go, Cyrano?" asked Mom.

"Who?"

"He's a character from a play who did some horrific matchmaking," she explained, opening the front door.

"Thank you for the vote of confidence," I said.

"Anything you say, Emma."

"*Who?*"

Mom swatted my butt. "We have *got* to buy you some classic literature."

Luckily, or maybe unluckily, when we got to the soccer field, Jefferson was sitting on the sidelines with his parents. While Mom set up her lawn chair nearby, I walked over to say hello.

Jefferson waved when he saw me approach. "Brooke, right?"

"Yeah, hi! Have you seen Lacey?"

"She's over there." He nodded to a group of girls in the center of the field.

"Great, thanks!" I turned to go but paused. "It's pretty cool that you watch your sister practice. My friend Tim plays baseball and—"

"I love baseball!" said Jefferson. "What position is he?"

"Uh . . . pitcher," I said. "Anyway, whenever he has a game—"

Jefferson blushed and smiled. "Sure. I'd love to go."

"You . . ." I leaned closer and blinked. "Sorry?"

He leaned in too, face fixed in an arrogant smirk. "I'd love to go to a game with you."

Whoa!

I stumbled back a few paces. "Uh . . . but you . . . tonight . . ." I pointed at him, shaking my finger like more words might shoot out.

"Tonight?" Jefferson shrugged. "Sure."

I squinted at him. "Really? You don't have plans?"

He waved a dismissive hand. "Nothing I can't cancel. When should we meet?"

What a slimeball!

"How about at half past get over yourself?" I fumed. "You have a date with Gabby, you jerk!"

Everyone on the field turned to look at me.

It was a tiny bit possible I'd said too much too loudly.

Jefferson recoiled. "What? How did you . . . Why did you . . ."

Too late to turn back now.

"Gabby wanted to know what you thought of her," I said. "Now I can tell her. So thanks for that!"

I stormed away, but when Mom sat up in her lawn chair to watch me, I shot her a panicked look.

"How goes the matchmaking?" she asked with a wry smile.

"Oh, *great*," I said, dropping onto the grass beside her. "I managed to get Gabby's date canceled." I chanced a peek in his direction and saw both him and Lacey glaring at me. "Also, I may have made an enemy of one of my teammates."

Coach blew the whistle, calling us all to the field.

"Good luck out there!" said Mom. "And I

hope you and Lacey are on the same side during the scrimmage."

We weren't.

Lacey's team won the kickoff, and while she waited for the ball to be passed to her, she caught my eye and drew a finger across her neck.

I was dead. Lovely.

Instead of coming at me, Lacey darted to one side and expertly maneuvered the ball past the right winger and a midfielder.

While our midfielders gave chase and the defensive players attempted to block Lacey, I bounced from foot to foot, waiting for my team to win the ball back. One of the sweepers got it away from Lacey and crossed it to me. I pivoted on one foot and ran the ball toward our goal, but one of *their* midfielders barred my path. With a quick sidelong glance, I saw that my left winger was open, and I arced the ball toward her at the same moment that Lacey hooked her left ankle around my right.

I tumbled forward, skidding across the grass on my hands and knees. Coach blew the whistle, and everyone trotted to a stop. I inspected my palms, which were streaked with grass stains, and my knees, which were somehow both green *and* a raw red. I winced as I wiped the grass away.

"That's a foul, Lacey," said Coach. "This time it's a warning; next time it's a yellow card."

Lacey didn't look even the tiniest bit bothered by this *or* by the fact that her foul earned me a penalty kick.

I placed the ball on its mark while the other team's keeper readied herself in front of the goal. Her fingers flexed in her gloves, and she nodded to Coach. He blew the whistle again, and I backed up a few paces and then charged the ball, angling my foot to feint like I was bending the strike to the left. The keeper leaned her body in that direction, poised to block.

At the last minute I straightened my foot

and drove the ball straight down the middle. The keeper couldn't correct her position quick enough, and the ball whizzed past her hip.

Coach tweeted the whistle. "Goal!"

The girls on my team cheered and slapped me on the back while Lacey fumed. For the rest of the first half, she dogged me. She didn't attempt any more intentional trippings, but she did her best to make it clear she had a score to settle.

At the end of the half, Coach blew the whistle, and we all dashed off the field to guzzle drinks from our sports bottles. Instead of heading toward Mom, I followed Lacey.

"Hey!" I jabbed her in the shoulder with my fingertips. "What's your problem?"

Lacey whirled to face me. "My problem? You were being a jerk to my brother! I thought you deserved a taste of your own medicine."

I glared at her. "Well, revenge looks great on you. Thanks for that free goal, by the way." I gave her a thumbs-up and started to leave. I paused, though, and said over my shoulder, "Your brother was going to hurt a really nice girl because a better offer came along. I know you would've yelled at him too."

Lacey didn't respond, and I trudged over to Mom who was waiting for me with a high-five.

"Nice first half!" she said, handing me a peeled orange.

"Thanks!" I ripped off a piece and practically swallowed it whole.

"How are your battle wounds?" She inspected my knees while I ate. "That girl really took you out," she said, clucking her tongue.

"I'm okay. If I wanted a no-contact sport, I would've taken up badminton."

"Or bowling," said another voice.

I grinned and turned around. "Dad!" I jumped up into his arms for a hug. "You made it!"

"Of course!" he said, hugging me back. "On

my list of things to do, this was high priority. I heard you scored a goal."

I nodded and filled him in.

He whistled and shook his head. "It's a cut-throat world, U12 soccer."

"Yeah, but I'm tough." I flexed both arms like a bodybuilder.

Dad held an orange up to one of my biceps. "Impressive! I remember when these guns were grape-sized."

I laughed and hung out with my parents until the break was over. Then Coach blew his whistle, and I headed back out for the second half. This time, Lacey was less aggressive, but she still had fire in her eyes, and when she bumped me to the ground, she didn't even glance back.

No Most Congenial trophy for her.

By the end of the game I was exhausted, and the thought of showering, dressing up, and walking to Heather's for pizza and movies was just too much. Plus, I still had homework and a history project to work on, and I hadn't yet picked my first letter for the advice column. It needed to be a good one to make people forget Friday's video fiasco.

"Awww!" said Vanessa when I conferenced in her and Heather to tell them. "But Musketeer Movies!"

"Next week will be superawesome Musketeer Movies," I promised. "But tonight I won't be good company. And people would ask why I'm walking down the street in my pajamas."

"You could say it's the new style," she suggested.

"No, *you* could say it's the new style. *And* get away with it," I said. "But my kittens-in-night-caps pattern won't fool anyone."

Heather giggled and said, "We'll miss you!"

"I'll miss you guys too! See you Monday!"

We got off the phone, and I started tackling

my homework. I went to bed early again, and on Sunday, Dad thought it would be a good idea for us to visit the Field Museum in Chicago so I could learn about ancient cultures firsthand.

Apparently, the Mesopotamians were big into wrestling and boxing, but I wasn't sure that would translate well to video and not look like regular fighting. They were also into dancing and music, but that was pretty much the same for any society, even today. I decided on a board game that the Mesopotamians had played called the Royal Game of Ur and went to work making my own board. And since organized astrology began in Babylonia, I also decided to make an astrology chart.

On Monday, I proudly showed it to Gil in Journalism, since he did the astrology section of the paper. He studied it and shook his head.

"I know the drawings aren't great," I said, "but—"

"It's not that," he said. "You're using our modern signs. The Babylonians also had a thirteenth sign: Ophiuchus." He flipped over my paper and started sketching on the back. "The zodiac is based on twelve constellations that appear in twelve evenly distributed sectors that the sun passes through in a year."

"So where's Oph . . . the thirteenth sign?" I asked.

"Ophiuchus is actually wedged between Scorpio and Sagittarius, but because it isn't visible for very long, it was left out over time." He moved his hand so I could see what he was drawing. "And so you get Ophiuchus, the serpent holder."

"That's so cool," I said, taking the paper from him. "Thanks!"

"Any time," he said.

I went to go sit with the other advice columnists, who had their heads close together in earnest conversation.

"What's going on?" I asked.

They parted to let me in, and I could see that Heather was shredding the edges of a piece of spiral paper with a guilty expression.

"It's all my fault," she said. "I never should have encouraged her."

"Who are we talking about?" I asked.

Tim turned to me with a troubled expression. "My sister. That guy Jefferson never met her at the movies."

Whoops. After the excitement of the game, I'd completely forgotten to tell Gabby what happened.

I sucked in air through my clenched teeth. "Actually, Heather didn't screw up. I may have had something to do with that."

The other three exchanged mystified looks. "What do you mean?"

I sighed. "He stood Gabby up after I asked him out."

"What?" Tim got to his feet, and I immediately raised my hands.

"It's not what you think! Gabby wanted to know what Jefferson thought of her, so I told him you play baseball, and he assumed I was asking him to a game—" I tried to rush through the explanation before Tim's head exploded all over my desk.

"You brought me into it?" His jaw dropped.

"It *is* my fault!" Heather threw little pieces of paper in the air. "I'm the one who told you to mention Tim!"

"What?" Tim spun around.

"I only mentioned you so I could bring up Gabby and see how Jefferson would respond!" I said. "As it turns out, the answer is badly."

Tim looked like he wanted to flip the table.

"Tim . . ."

"What?" This time he faced Vanessa, who gave him an indignant look.

"Uh . . . no, sir. You are getting way too much mileage out of that word," she said. "And you need to calm down." She pointed to his chair.

Tim sat but continued to seethe.

"You know Heather and Brooke would never do anything to hurt Gabby on purpose."

I nodded so hard my teeth ached. "I was wiped out after the scrimmage and completely forgot to call Gabby and tell her what happened." I held up a finger. "*But* I did yell at Jefferson when he wanted to go out with me instead of her."

Tim shook his head. "All I know is that my sister is crushed. Would you let her know what really happened?"

"I think she already does," said Heather in a small voice.

We looked over at her, and her eyes were welling up with tears. She held out a piece of paper from the collection she'd just gathered from the advice box.

"What does it say?" I asked, taking it from her.

"'Dear Lincoln's Letters,'" I read. "'The *worst* thing has happened. I've been betrayed by my friends. I asked them for help with this guy I like, but all they did was make sure that he never talks to me again. Why would they do that?'" I sighed and lowered the paper. "'Sincerely, Betrayed in Berryville.'"

"We've gotta fix this," I said to Heather. "We see her next period. What should we tell her?"

"How about . . . the truth?" mumbled Vanessa through a mouthful of chocolate. She'd taken a king-size Hershey bar out of her bag so we could console ourselves.

"Uh-oh," said Tim in a low voice. "Don't look now, but Mary Patrick's coming!"

I pointed to Vanessa. "Quick! Distract her with chocolate!"

"Gah!" Vanessa lobbed the candy bar at Mary

Patrick as if it were a grenade.

I stared at her. "Really."

Vanessa blinked at me. "I didn't have time to prop a box up with a stick and build a Mary Patrick trap." She nodded at Mary Patrick, who had crouched to retrieve the chocolate. "Besides, she's still taking the bait."

"Thirty-second rule," said Mary Patrick with a shrug. "I know it's supposed to be five seconds, but I make an exception for chocolate."

"What's going on?" I asked her.

Mary Patrick picked a piece of lint off the candy. "I'm surprised you're not all racing to the front to see the first issue of the *Lincoln Log.* Most newbies usually do."

I glanced at my teammates in confusion.

"The short issue? Why would we care? We're not in it."

It was Mary Patrick's turn to look confused. "Mrs. H gave me your pieces last Friday, and they went to the printers, along with everything else."

Instantly, our table was abuzz.

"What pieces?" demanded Tim.

"We didn't turn in any pieces!" I added.

"Are you sure they were *our* pieces?" asked Heather.

"She didn't take the pieces from the video, did she?" Vanessa clapped a hand to her forehead.

Mary Patrick thrust out her hands to silence us. "Everyone stop saying *pieces*! It's making me think of Reese's Pieces and the fact that I don't have any!"

Mrs. H hurried over. "What is all the fuss about, staffers? This is highly unprofessional newsroom behavior."

"Mary Patrick said you turned in our advice column on Friday, but we didn't give you any material," I told her.

She smiled and opened her arms with a

flourish. "Surprise! We were going to wait until the first full week of school, but after that video . . . mishap"—she smiled politely—"I thought it might be better to show you've got what it takes *now*. So I used your practice material that Mary Patrick shared from the second day of class!" Mrs. H cocked her head. "You don't seem as happy as I thought you'd be."

Heather cleared her throat. "I think we wanted a little more time to—"

"You published my Sir Stinks a Lot piece?" Tim's voice came out as a squeak. "That was meant to be funny!"

"And it was!" Mrs. H placed a reassuring hand on his shoulder. "But it was also sound advice."

He sighed and banged his forehead on the desk. "Ow."

"Mrs. H is right," I said. "Even though they were just practice, we still did a good job. And our column can use all the positive exposure it can get." I nodded approvingly.

"Glad you feel that way!" she said, beaming. "Because I thought it might be nice to have our staffers personally distribute this issue."

She beckoned across the room, where two guys waited with stacks of newspapers wrapped in twine. One of them grabbed a bundle in each hand and made his way to our table.

Despite our earlier cries of protest, Tim, Heather, Vanessa, and I couldn't help staring in awe. The smell of the news ink hit me, and I wriggled a copy of the *Lincoln Log* out from under the twine.

"Guys, we're in here," I said in a voice barely above a whisper. "Our names in print."

"Well, don't just stare at the headlines. Find our page!" Vanessa spread the paper on the table, and we all lunged for it at once.

"Careful!" said Heather. "You'll rip it."

The paper rustled as I searched and finally

spotted the corner of Gil's horoscope, which meant . . .

"Our column!" I crowed, smoothing the pages flat.

"Look, there's me!" Vanessa jabbed at her name. "Ooh, I've got to get a pic of this!" She reached for her purse, but Mrs. H stopped her.

To be honest, I'd momentarily forgotten she was there.

"I'll be sure to save a few copies for you to take home to your parents," Mrs. H said with a smile. "For now, let's focus on this week's advice, and I'll give you time at the end of class to hand out the *Lincoln Log*."

"I'm going to work on an answer for Gabby," Heather informed us, putting pencil to notebook.

Vanessa started dividing up the advice requests, and I flipped each one over, inspecting both sides.

"What are you doing?" she asked.

"Nothing," I said, dropping the piece I was holding. But I continued to eye each slip of paper as she moved it across the table.

"She's looking for something," said Tim, regarding me with the same intensity I'd been using for the advice requests. Then, his expression cleared and he grinned. "Oh, I know what it is."

"What?" Vanessa asked.

"I'm betting a certain secret admirer didn't leave her a note this morning," he said with a smirk.

"Awww!" Heather looked up from her writing. "He didn't?"

Three sets of eyes were on me. I squirmed and made a face. "Pfft. I don't know. I didn't check. I don't care. Whatever."

I knew. I'd checked. And as much as I hated to admit it, I cared.

My secret admirer hadn't left me a note.

"Maybe he found out about you and Jefferson," said Tim, clapping a hand to his cheek in mock surprise. "Scandalous!"

I glowered at him. "You're enjoying this too much."

"Well, if he's the kind of guy who listens to gossip, Brooke doesn't need him, anyway," said Heather, giving me a reassuring smile. "Now, tell me what you guys think of this response. 'Dear Betrayed in Berryville, I'm sorry for what happened. Really, truly. I can't apologize enough for what—"

"Um . . ." I put a hand on Heather's arm. "We chased off her date; we didn't kill him."

Heather gave me puppy dog eyes. "But I'm really sorry for what happened!"

"I am too," I said. "But these are supposed to be anonymous, and Gabby can't know that we know."

She sniffled. "You're right. Plus, it's probably better if we apologize in person."

"Okay, so skip the 'I'm sorry' part," Tim suggested. "And get to the advice."

Heather nodded. "Let's see . . ." She ran her finger down the page before flipping it over.

"Wow," said Vanessa. "You were insanely sorry."

Heather stuck her tongue out at her. "Here we go. 'If they're good friends, they probably had the best intentions, but sometimes even those can go wrong. Try talking to them to get the whole story. I'm sure you're only hearing half of it, maybe less. And don't worry, if this guy is really worth it, he'll give you a second chance. Everyone makes mistakes. Confidentially yours, Heather.'"

Tim, Vanessa, and I applauded, and Heather beamed.

"Who's next?" she asked.

"Here's a good one for Brooke." Vanessa waved a slip at me. "Some kid sprained his ankle so he can't play sports until it heals."

"Which is why sports video games were invented," said Tim.

She smirked. "Anyway, he's asking if there are any sports that don't require him to be on his feet."

"Sure," I said with a shrug. "People in wheelchairs play soccer, basketball—"

"Even rugby," added Tim. "Although, that might result in more injuries. That sport's brutal!"

I started crafting my response but paused. "Do you really think my secret admirer stopped writing because of Jefferson?"

My friends all groaned.

"What brought that up?" asked Vanessa.

"Sports, guys, my secret admirer's a guy, I wonder if he likes sports, I wonder if he likes me," I said, laying out my thought process.

"Makes sense," said Heather.

"Does it really matter?" asked Tim. "You don't even know who this guy is. It might not even be a guy! It could be the lunch lady."

The rest of us stared him down.

He shifted in his seat. "Or . . . it might be the cutest guy in school who's also an actor and raises money to help needy sea otters."

Heather patted him on the hand. "Maybe just stop."

"Why don't you write a note to your secret admirer?" suggested Vanessa. "He always puts his in the advice box. We could leave it unlocked, and you could leave a note for him to find."

"That's not a bad idea," I said.

"That's a terrible idea!" said Tim. "You're turning this into a bigger deal than it is, and you're going to scare him off."

"I like it," spoke up Heather. "It takes a lot of

courage to talk to someone you're interested in." Her gaze wandered past Tim, to where Stefan stood talking to Mrs. H.

The only one who looked over was Mrs. H, who smiled, glanced at her watch, and approached our table.

"Are we ready to get these to our readers?" She patted one of the newspaper bundles, and all four of us nodded. "Great! Heather and Tim, why don't you take the east side of the sixth grade hall while Brooke and Vanessa take the west?"

"You got it," said Tim, taking a bundle and gesturing to Heather. "After you."

I picked up the other bundle and carried it in both arms. The advice, and my secret admirer, would have to wait for now. "You ready for potential ridicule and shame?" I asked Vanessa. "You're with the Booger Eater, you know."

"Booger Eater and Blank Stare," she said with a grin. "When you need a crime to *not* be solved, you know who to call!"

I laughed and led the way down the hall. At the first classroom, Vanessa knocked on the door and poked her head in.

"Special delivery!" she said.

I snipped the twine with a pair of scissors and started passing out copies, greeting everyone with a big smile.

"Hi, how are you? Check out the advice column, it's pretty awesome."

"Do you give advice on how to eat boogers?" a guy wearing a basketball jersey asked.

Several people laughed.

"Do you give advice on terrible sports teams to follow?" I asked, gesturing to his jersey.

Several people said, "Oooh!"

"Nobody wants to play for the Kings. Not even the Kings," I said. "How much did they pay you to wear that?"

"I told you!" The guy sitting behind him said

gleefully, popping him in the shoulder.

The guy in the jersey sneered at me. "Like you know anything about sports."

"I play soccer and coed baseball, and watch basketball, football, and golf," I informed him. "You think you can stump me with something? Write in to the advice column."

"I will!" he said, opening up his notebook and scribbling on a sheet of paper.

While I was busy not making friends, Vanessa had attracted a small group.

"Don't worry, people," I said. "There's plenty of news for—" The cluster of students opened to let me in.

Vanessa had managed to get her head trapped under a chair.

I widened my eyes. "What happened?"

"I think it's gum!" she called back in a muffled voice. "I dropped a paper under here and . . . Could you just get me out?"

"Sure," I said, "but you're not gonna like it."

Grabbing the same pair of scissors I'd used to cut the twine, I snipped her hair free of the gum under the chair.

"Thank goodness for hats," she said, making a face and rubbing her freshly cut hair.

We worked our way through ten more classrooms and made our way back to the main hall just as the bell rang. Vanessa and I gave each other a triumphant high five and headed for our next classes.

Heather was pacing outside the door to our history classroom when I showed up.

"Is Gabby in there?" I poked my head around the corner.

"Not yet. Have you thought about what you're going to tell her?"

"Yep. You?"

She nodded. "Let's talk to her out here, though. We don't want the whole room to hear and make this more embarrassing than it has to be."

"Good idea." Heather and I leaned against the wall. "How did the newspaper handout go?"

Her troubled expression lightened. "Really well! Tim kept cracking jokes, and people even made us wait around so they could read our advice in person. How about you?"

"I gave Vanessa an impromptu haircut."

She raised her eyebrows. "Good . . . job?"

We stood around until the crowd in the hall thinned to just a few students running to beat the bell. Finally, Mr. Costas called to us.

"Inside and close the door, girls!"

I glanced at Gabby's desk to see if she'd slipped past us, but it was empty.

"Where's Gabby?"

Mr. Costas frowned. "She wasn't feeling well, so her mom came and picked her up last period."

"Awww," said Heather.

"It's okay. She can't avoid us forever," I said.

Heather went to join her group, and I joined mine, telling them about my board game and showing them the horoscope chart I'd drawn for the sports and leisure portion of our project.

"What about your other topics?" asked my teammate Spencer.

"My . . ." I cringed. I'd forgotten I was supposed to cover food, money, and medicine, too. "I left the rest of that stuff at home," I said. "The food and medicine might have spoiled, and the money . . . uh"—I cleared my throat and whispered—"counterfeiting is illegal!"

Spencer gave me a strange look. "Anyway. Here's what I made for the language bit. It's cuneiform." He pulled out a tablet-sized piece of clay with indentations in it.

"That's awesome!" I said. "Does this actually spell anything?" I ran my fingertips over all the bumps and ridges.

Spencer grinned sheepishly. "It says 'Vote Spencer for Sixth-Grade President.' I'm running for student council."

"Student council!" I snapped my fingers. "I completely forgot I wanted to do that. Thanks for the reminder!"

"You're welcome," he said, shifting his gaze to the floor. "What . . . uh . . . what position?"

"Nothing but the best," I said. "Sixth-grade president, of course! May the best candidate win!" I punched him in the arm.

"Yeah," he said, rubbing it.

"Um . . . so Spencer, how long did it take you to make this?" asked Ashley, the other girl in our group.

"Almost my entire Saturday," he confessed. "But it was fun." He showed us the rest of the stuff he'd completed, and then Ashley shared her sections.

I watched and marveled at their hard work,

feeling like the biggest jerk for being the only one who hadn't come through on the deadline *I'd* made. I had to make up for this failure!

"Okay," I told them in my most serious voice. "Let's schedule a date to get our video complete. What's everyone's schedules like?"

"I'm free all week except Thursday," said Spencer.

"Me too," said Ashley.

I'm not gonna lie; I envied them.

"I have soccer all this week except Wednesday," I said, "so why don't we put our video together then?"

They nodded.

"Great! Hand in all your research to me tomorrow, and I'll put together a script."

"Are you sure?" asked Ashley. "I can—"

I waved a dismissive hand. "I got it."

At the end of class, Heather left her group to talk to me.

"Do you think Gabby's okay?" she asked.

"If she wasn't, Tim would've said something, right?" I asked. "Besides, I've got bigger things to focus on. Like this project. Oh! And I'm running for president!"

She smiled. "I think you've got a few years before you're ready for the White House."

"No!" I laughed. "Of the sixth grade!"

"Oh!" She giggled too. "Well, if you need any help with your campaign, let me know. Also, I'm going to the library tonight," she said. "You should come with me."

"I don't have time," I said with a sigh. "I have soccer."

Heather shrugged. "Then we'll go after soccer. I'll come with you!"

I looked up from my notebook. "Really? You want to watch me practice?"

None of my friends ever wanted to do that.

Heather smiled. "Don't act so surprised! I miss hanging out."

"Awww!" I gave her a spontaneous hug. "I know, me too! Things are just so crazy right now."

"Tell me about it." She rolled her eyes. "The choral director at this school is insane. She wants us to spend fifteen minutes a day singing."

I frowned. "That's not so bad."

"While running on a treadmill."

"Ha! Where are you supposed to get a treadmill?" I asked.

Heather bumped me toward the door. "*That's* the part you have questions about?"

She and I talked all the way to Mom's car and then all the way to the soccer field. I couldn't believe how much I'd missed in just a week.

"They offered you a solo and you turned it down?" I asked. "But you're so good!"

"Thanks," she said with a modest smile. "But a solo means standing alone, with all eyes on me." Heather shuddered. "That's too much pressure."

I goggled at her. "Last Friday you spoke to the entire school during our Meet the Press video."

"That was different! I was talking to a video camera," she said.

"So pretend everyone at the concert is a giant video camera," I said.

"Right. Because that's not creepy."

I poked Mom in the shoulder. "You agree with me, right?"

She chuckled. "I agree that Heather has a beautiful singing voice, but if she isn't ready, she isn't ready."

"Thank you, Mrs. Jacobs!" Heather said, giving me an I-told-you-so look.

I snorted. "That is so not my approach to life. My motto is 'Ready or not, here I come!'"

Heather tilted her head to one side. "I'm pretty sure that's wrong."

Mom pulled up to the curb by the soccer field. "Brooke, stop bullying Heather. And have fun at practice. Do you need me to pick you up later?"

"We're going to the library after," I told her. "I'll call you from there."

I kissed Mom on the cheek, and Heather waved to her as we both hopped out.

"I'm so excited to see you play!" said Heather.

"Jacobs!"

I turned just as Coach threw a cloth bundle at me. I gasped and opened it.

"Is this . . . ? It is! Our new uniform!"

I held it up and admired the bright colors and fresh scent that was completely without body odor.

"It works better as clothing than decoration,"

said Coach with a smile. "Get changed and on the field."

Heather and I ran into the women's locker room, where I changed and preened momentarily in front of the mirror.

"I love it!" I said, beaming.

"Let me get a pic." Heather pulled out her phone, and I posed. "Perfect!"

"Okay, now I really have to get to practice," I said with a giggle.

Heather took my bag of school clothes. "I'll go find a place to sit."

I pointed to one of the shade trees. "My mom always sits over there where . . . ugh . . . Jefferson is."

We both made sour milk faces.

"I think I'll stay as far from him as possible," said Heather. She grabbed my arm. "Hey, look! It's Gabby! We can apologize in person!"

"Oh?" I said, following her gaze. "Oh!" I looked

at the big white bucket in Gabby's hand. "Ohhh."
I watched as she stormed toward Jefferson. "Oh,
oh, oh!" I tugged on Heather's arm. "We have to
stop her!"

"What?" Heather yelled, running after me.

I had no idea what was in the bucket, but I
was betting it wasn't butterflies and confetti.

Do or Dye

"Gabby!" I shouted her name, hoping she'd freeze in her tracks.

She did, for just a second, but then doubled her pace toward Jefferson. I needed to change tactics.

I imagined that Gabby was a striker, the mystery bucket was a soccer ball, and Jefferson was the goal.

No way could I let her score that point.

I put on a burst of speed and reached Gabby just as she hoisted the bucket onto one shoulder.

"Don't!" I yanked on her arm. "Jefferson, move!"

Of course he had his earbuds in, completely oblivious to the world.

Gabby must have been running on adrenaline because she tore herself free of my grasp, purple goop sloshing over the rim of the bucket.

"Stop!" Heather finally caught up, but instead of going for Gabby's arms, she grabbed for her waist.

Gabby twisted and lurched forward as the bucket on her shoulder tipped backward.

Heather and I screamed and tried to escape by running.

Toward each other.

We did not get far.

Gallons of purple goo crashed down on us like a thick, sticky tidal wave. Beside me, Heather whimpered while I fought to wipe goo out of my eyes.

"What the heck is this stuff?" I screeched.

"It's grape snow-cone syrup from my cousin's

shop!" I heard Gabby say. "I'm so sorry! I have to—"

She stopped talking, and I squinted through syrup, waving my arms in front of me. "Gabby?"

From out of nowhere, hands appeared with towels, and I could hear a myriad of voices.

"*What* happened?"

"Are you okay?"

"Here. Get your face first."

"Watch out, that stuff'll stain!"

I took a towel and wiped down my face, then used it to squeeze the syrup out of my hair. Each section stuck out from my head, so I felt like a purple porcupine. I exchanged an annoyed look with Heather and studied the crowd gathered around us. Parents, my teammates, Jefferson, but no Gabby. All that remained of her was the white plastic bucket tossed to the side.

Coach managed to break his way through the crowd.

"Are you girls okay?"

Heather and I nodded. My hair and skin were quickly stiffening, and I could feel syrup trickling into my uniform.

My uniform!

I gasped long and loud.

"What? What is it?" Heather grabbed my shoulders, her slimy palms squishing against the fabric.

"I . . . My . . ." I pointed to my clothes.

Coach shook his head. "I'm pretty sure they're ruined, but go shower off, anyway." To the rest of my teammates he said, "Way to hustle and look out for one of your own. Now it's time to get to work." He blew a whistle, and they all sprinted onto the field.

I disappeared into the locker room with Heather.

"Ugh! Can you believe Gabby?" I groaned with exasperation and slammed a purple towel into the trash can. "Come on." I pulled her toward the showers. "Let's see if this stuff washes out."

We approached two empty stalls and looked at each other.

"See you on the other side," I said, pulling back the curtain and stepping in fully clothed. Heather did the same in the next one.

A minute later twin clouds of steam were coming out of our showers, but no purple was coming out of my clothes.

"Brooke? It isn't working!" Heather shouted to me.

"I know!" I shouted back.

"Well, that's one outfit that won't survive the school year," she said, turning off her water.

I didn't answer, too busy squirting soap from a dispenser directly onto my jersey. I scrubbed until my fingers hurt and my skin was wrinkled from being waterlogged. But my uniform was ruined.

Shoulders slumped, I turned off my own shower and squeezed water out of my clothes and ponytail.

When I stepped out, Heather was waiting with towels wrapped around her head and fully clothed body. Ordinarily, I might've said she looked ridiculous, but I looked like a giant raisin, so I had no room to talk.

"Oh, Brooke! I'm so sorry about your pretty new uniform." She handed me a clean dry towel and hugged me. When she stepped back, she was frowning. "Uh-oh."

"What-oh?" I asked.

Heather chewed her lip. "You're no longer a . . . pure redhead."

I groaned and grabbed the end of my ponytail, pulling it in front of my face. Red streaked with purple.

"This is *not* a good combination," I muttered.

"But Heather, you were directly behind Gabby. You know what that means?" I nodded to the turban on her head.

Heather's eyes widened, and she spun toward the mirror, pulling off her hair towel in the process.

"Ahhhh!" she shrieked, tugging at her deep purple hair. "My parents are going to kill me!"

I pulled her hair back. "It's not that bad! Your hair is dark so it doesn't show as much."

"It shows enough!" she informed me. "We have school tomorrow *and* I have Hebrew school after that! Oy vey!"

"It's okay, I can fix this. Just . . ." I covered her head with my towel. "Better."

"Thanks," she muttered through the cloth.

"That's not my solution!" I said. "But your head is distracting me. I need to think."

Heather found her purse and took out her phone. "No, you need to call your mom and have her take us to Vanessa's." She pressed the phone firmly into my hand. "We need professional help."

As much as I hated to miss practice, Heather had a point. And I couldn't really abandon her since the problem with Gabby was 90 percent my fault. After I called Mom, I changed into the old uniform I still had in my bag and lent my school clothes to Heather.

When we walked out of the clubroom, Coach closed his eyes and sighed before opening them.

"How much trouble will you be in for coloring your hair?"

"We didn't color it," I said. "G— Someone else did."

Even though I was furious at her, on the off-chance that nobody had figured out who Gabby was, her identity might as well stay a secret.

"The girl who fled the scene?" he asked.

Heather and I nodded.

"What exactly happened?" asked Coach.

We explained, and when we were done, I blushed and said, "So if it's okay, I have to miss practice today."

"Of course." Coach motioned for me to have a seat on the grass. "Since you're taking off early I want to show you something." He reached for his clipboard. "Here's your current ranking."

I smiled modestly in anticipation of what was to come, ready to shoo off any compliments Coach gave. But as soon as I took the clipboard I dropped it like a hot coal.

"What?" I squeaked. "I'm ranked third?"

"Third is good!" Heather said with a reassuring smile. "It's still a medal in the Olympics."

"Third is quite admirable," Coach agreed. "Your main area of opportunity is that you don't run the plays properly. I gave you several different plays to run yesterday, and you only did half."

"But I made goals, anyway!"

Coach didn't look convinced. "That's not the point. I need you to run the plays just as the other girls are. If you're out there doing your own thing, it's not a cohesive team effort."

"I guess," I mumbled.

"It's easy to get back on top of the ranking. Keep playing well *and* follow instructions." He tapped me on the knee with the clipboard. "Now take the night off to absorb this." He glanced at my hair. "Like it's snow-cone syrup."

When Mom pulled up, she took one look at Heather and me and covered her mouth with her hand, but I could see a smile peeking out from behind it.

"Don't laugh," I said with a scowl. "Or say 'I told you so' or ask if I had a *grape* day."

Mom pressed her lips together. "Actually," she said with a waver in her voice, "I was going to say you look . . . *mauve*lous."

There was a choking sound from behind me,

and I looked back to see Heather trying very hard not to laugh. I narrowed my eyes at her but couldn't help smiling.

"Don't make me happy," I said. "I'm having a bad day."

I told her about what Coach had said, but instead of getting angry for me, Mom just chuckled.

"What?" I asked.

"It's just funny that you expect people to take your advice but you refuse to take theirs."

"Not when it doesn't make sense!" I said. "Why should I follow Coach's plays when I know what I'm doing?"

"Because he's the coach!" Mom and Heather said in unison.

All three of us laughed.

"The reason is right in the job title," Mom added. "Believe it or not, there might be one or two people out there who know stuff you don't."

"Wha?" I feigned disbelief. "Impossible!"

My phone dinged with a new text from Tim.

Gabby just got home crying about you and Heather. What happened?

I had no desire to get into it with him. I typed back:

Can't talk. On the way to Vanessa's.

"Brooke? Are you listening?" asked Mom, stopping at a red light. "It's one thing to give advice; it's another to try and fix the problem yourself."

"That should be a rule," I told Heather.

Her eyes lit up, and she pulled out her phone, tapping away at the keys. "We need to start making a list of rules for the advice column. Rule number one: give advice but don't interfere."

"Rule number two: Some people are beyond help," I added.

"Oh, I don't believe that," said Heather. "Some people just need extra help."

"Like a straitjacket."

Heather swatted me. "Rule number three: don't make fun of the people seeking advice. They were brave enough to ask."

I snorted. "If Gabby had really been brave, she would've asked Jefferson how he felt herself." Heather started to interrupt, but I held up a finger. "And if she didn't like the answer, she would've confronted him face-to-face, not bucket-to-back."

"I disagree," said Mom from the front seat. "That's how *you* would've reacted, but clearly that's not Gabby's personality."

Heather started typing on her phone. "Rule number four: One answer does not fit all. Offer more than one solution to the problem."

Heather and I came up with a couple more rules, like rule #5: keep the advice upbeat, before we reached Vanessa's driveway. She was already waiting outside with her little brother, Terrell, and when I hopped out, he was as polite as any six-year-old would be.

"Whoa! What happened to your head?" he squeaked. "You look like an eggplant."

"Terrell!" Vanessa bumped him. "Go back inside." She smiled and waved at my mom. "Hi, Mrs. Jacobs."

Mom smiled at her. "I hope you can help these girls."

"And quick," said Heather. "I don't want to look like this at school tomorrow."

"That's too bad," said Vanessa, linking her arm through Heather's. "Because I think you look cute."

Mom and I followed them into the house, where Mrs. Jackson greeted us and offered coffee to Mom and cake to all of us.

"Good luck!" Mom called after Heather, Vanessa, and me.

"If you shave their heads, I wanna help!" shouted Terrell.

Vanessa led us into the bathroom, where a box of bottles and tubes was sitting on the counter.

"Neutralizers, cleansers, and colors," she explained when Heather and I eyed the container suspiciously. "If it doesn't wash out or fade, we'll dye your hair back to its original color."

Since Heather was more worried than I was, Vanessa went to work on her first. After scrubbing and soaking, she'd gotten rid of most of the color, but there was still a slight tinge to it.

"Well." Vanessa wiped at her forehead, smearing soapsuds across it. "If you want, we can dye it. That'll definitely hide the rest of the color."

Heather studied her reflection in the mirror. "No."

Vanessa and I looked at each other, then at Heather.

"What?" I asked.

Heather smiled. "Now that it's not as obvious, I kinda like it."

Vanessa pulled out a hair dryer. "Me too!"

She gave Heather a quick blowout and turned to me. "You're next!"

Vanessa put an old towel around my shoulders and set to work with the neutralizer while I sat on the closed toilet. From somewhere nearby, I heard the doorbell chime. Vanessa paused in her work.

"Who's that?"

A couple minutes later we had our answer. Tim appeared at the top of the stairs with Gabby. Her hands were in her pockets, and her head was bowed.

"Hey, can we come in?" asked Tim.

Vanessa glanced around. "If one of you wants to stand in the bathtub, sure."

Tim laughed until Vanessa moved a shampoo bottle out of the way.

"Oh, you're serious." He climbed in.

Gabby approached the bathroom door, but I

thrust out a halting hand.

"Wait. Are you armed? Turn out your pockets."

"Brooke!" Heather nudged me.

"I don't want to be any other colors!" I told her.

Gabby blushed but showed us her empty pockets. Then she continued to just stand there.

Tim cleared his throat. "On top of making an excellent statue, my sister *also* has something to say. Don't make me poke you with this back scrubber," he said, waving the brush at her.

Gabby took a deep breath, and the intake of air seemed to push tears out of her eyes.

"I just wanted to say I'm sorry again."

And then she let out all the air, along with almost every word in the human language.

"I'm so embarrassed and I don't know what I was thinking and I'm so glad you stopped me from making an even bigger fool of myself. I was so hurt that he didn't want to go out with me and I shouldn't have asked either of you to get involved and I promise I'll pay to have your uniform replaced"—that comment was directed at me—"and I think you look really good with purple highlights"—directed at Heather.

Gabby took another deep breath, but before she could continue, Heather stopped her with a light touch to the arm.

"I get that you were upset," she said. "But there has to be a better way to deal with it."

Gabby nodded and smiled shyly. "I actually came up with something that'll help not just me, but other girls."

"That's great!" I said.

"And we're sorry too," added Heather. "We saw your request to 'Lincoln's Letters,' and we felt so terrible! We should never have interfered."

Then she leaned over and gave Gabby a big hug.

"My request?" Gabby looked over Heather's shoulder at me. I nodded.

"From Betrayed in Berryville?" I said.

Gabby shook her head. "No idea what you're talking about."

I clapped my hand to my forehead. "So there's potentially another girl out there running around with a bucket of snow-cone syrup?"

The others laughed.

"We forgive you," I told Gabby, smiling. "And we've made it a 'Lincoln's Letters' rule not to do anything more than give advice."

"We have rules?" asked Tim.

"Yeah, when did this happen?" asked Vanessa.

Heather and I went over the list we'd started.

"And rule number six: If people ask for advice but don't take it, don't get mad," finished Heather.

"To go along with that, I think we should add

another one," I said. "Rule number seven: never give up on people."

Heather smiled. "I like it!"

"Me too," said Vanessa.

"You know what this list needs?" asked Tim. "An official book!"

Vanessa snapped her fingers. "Be right back."

She squeezed past Heather, Gabby, and me and disappeared into her room, returning a minute later with a leather-bound journal. "Ta-da!" She held it up and showed us the empty pages. "I bought a couple of these for sketches, but I can sacrifice one for the greater good."

"Perfect!" Tim took it, along with a pen Vanessa offered. "What was rule number one?"

While Heather and I repeated the rules, Vanessa worked on my hair, and Gabby called her mom and begged for purple highlights. We all talked and laughed, and Mom and Mrs. Jackson ordered takeout and brought it up so we could eat. It was the oddest and only bathroom party I'd ever attended and the most fun I'd had since school started.

The only downside was that I'd missed soccer practice and a trip to the library for my history project.

But I still had plenty of time, right?

CHAPTER

8

Popular Opinion

When Mom dropped me off at school the next morning, Tim, Vanessa, and Heather were all waiting for me at the curb.

"Hey, guys!" I greeted them. "What's up?"

"Mary Patrick," said Tim, pointing a thumb over his shoulder.

"Uh-oh." I peered around him. "What'd she do now?"

"Just come with us," said Vanessa, hooking her arm through mine. "She refuses to speak to anyone but our section lead."

When we got closer to the building, I could

see Mary Patrick by the entrance, wearing a bright-yellow hard hat.

"Why is she dressed like a construction worker?" I asked Vanessa. "Did she hear how accident-prone you were?"

Vanessa shoved me.

"We think she's on some safety committee," said Heather.

"Or that she's just crazy," said Tim.

His guess turned out to be the closest.

When we approached her, Mary Patrick's eyes fixed on me.

"Finally," she said. "I was beginning to wonder if your team even knew who their section lead was!"

"You can talk to any of them at any time," I said. "What's with the Bob the Builder getup?"

"It's Toughen-Up Tuesday," said Mary Patrick, taking off the hard hat and plopping it on my head. "Toughen up!"

"Uh . . . why?" asked Heather.

"Because today is when you'll start receiving feedback about your first column," said Mary Patrick. "And it won't all be pretty."

"You don't know that," I said.

Mary Patrick gave me a sad smile. "Look inside the hat."

I turned it over to find pieces of paper taped inside.

"'Brooke Jacobs gives bad advice,'" I read.

"Oh boy," said Vanessa.

"'She's not a professional and doesn't know proper warm-up techniques'?" I lowered the paper. "My coach has us do those stretches before every practice! Why would you show me something so mean?"

Mary Patrick raised an eyebrow. "That's actually one of the nicer ones someone told me in person."

"In person?" asked Tim, taking the hard hat

from me. "Some people wrote in?"

Mary Patrick crossed her arms. "If you all bothered to read the entire paper and not just your own section, you would've seen a request for feedback to be dropped in the advice box."

"Um . . . excuse me. You went through our advice box?" asked Vanessa, hand on hip.

"Was there anything else in it?" I asked. I would die if she'd seen a note from my secret admirer.

"Anything else?" she repeated. "Advice requests, but I left them there. Why are you staring like that? Do I have something on my nose?"

"Who told you my warm-up advice was bad?" I asked.

"Abel Hart, but that doesn't matter," she said. "The point—"

"Yeah, you might as well save your breath." Vanessa patted Mary Patrick's shoulder. "Brooke has gone to her angry place."

"Brooke, sweetie?" Heather ventured. "If you kill him, you'll probably get detention."

"Abel Hart thinks I don't know?" I exploded. "*He* doesn't know!" I threw down the hard hat and stormed toward the cafeteria, the place I always saw him in the mornings.

"Wait! I'm not finished!" Mary Patrick called after me.

I found Abel sitting on a bench with his head tilted back and his big stupid mouth wide open, trying to catch home fries that another dumb goon was throwing at him. So much for the sophisticated Young Sherlock.

The next flying potato piece I snatched in midair.

"Hey!" Abel frowned at me. "I had that!"

I crushed the home fry in my fist, then offered him the paste. "Still want it?"

Abel looked from the potato shrapnel to me. "Well, I'm hungry, so . . ." He reached into my palm.

"Ew! Stop that!" I scraped off my hand and wiped it on my jeans. "And stop saying mean things about me!"

Abel blinked up at me. "I didn't say those mean things about your socks! I don't know where that rumor started."

"That's not what I—" I paused. "There's a rumor about my socks?" I glanced at my feet.

"Yeah, that you only have one pair." He looked down. "Because you only wear *that* pair."

"They're athletic socks. They all look like this."

"All . . . two of them?" he asked, raising an eyebrow.

I thumped him on the forehead. "I have a drawerful! And that's not why I'm here! You said I gave bad advice."

His forehead wrinkled for a second and then relaxed. "Oh, that! Yeah, you totally gave bad advice. If you stretch like that before you run long distance, you'll mess up your muscles."

"How would *you* know?"

"I run long distance," he said flatly. "Also, my dad is a sports physician. You should really do your research before you answer your questions. *And* if you want to make it in Young Sherlocks." He gestured to the guy who was throwing home fries and opened his mouth wide again.

I wedged a dirty napkin in between his teeth and walked away.

Heather and Vanessa were waiting for me in the hall.

"Sooo. That sounded like it went well," said Heather.

"He said I should do research!"

Heather and Vanessa looked at each other.

"I know," I said with a sigh. "When I say it out

loud, it does make sense."

"It's your first column," said Heather.

"We'll add that to our list of rules," said Vanessa. "Rule number eight: fact-check your advice whenever possible."

I sighed and trudged toward homeroom. "Mary Patrick said there were meaner ones than Abel's."

"I'm sure there were nicer ones too," said Heather.

And she was right.

In fact, a debate started in my PE class based on my column, with half the people on my side and half the people against. No doubt about it, words held power.

And apparently a certain attraction. In between each class, I saw Tim with at least one girl walking by his side, talking his ear off.

"I can't believe you quote Shakespeare!" one girl gushed. "You are so sophisticated."

I didn't bother interrupting to mention that Tim had been armpit fart champion on our coed baseball team.

Nobody seemed to argue with Vanessa's advice on fur since most kids at our school were of the same mind. She'd shown me her Toughen-Up feedback, which had simply been "I prefer feathers." And Heather's advice on friendship was nothing but friendly, so she had it easy.

For some reason the lack of feedback bothered both of them.

"I don't see what the big deal is," I told Vanessa when she met me at my locker for lunch. "You should be glad nobody has anything to say about you."

"Don't you get it? Great advice gets noticed and terrible advice gets noticed, but when readers don't have a strong opinion either way . . ." She shrugged. "Vanessa who?"

"You get plenty of attention," I said. "Your

fashion choices guarantee it. What do you call these, by the way?" I grabbed one of her sleeves, the bottom half of which was attached at the waist of her shirt. "You look like you're about to take flight."

Vanessa laughed. "They're called 'batwing sleeves,'" she said.

I grinned. "No way."

"Yes way!" She spread her arms wide. "Now, let's flap on down to the cafeteria."

I wrinkled my nose. "Pass. I need to practice soccer plays."

Vanessa wrinkled her forehead. "But . . . food." She pointed to her stomach.

"But . . . wannabe team captain." I pointed to myself. "If I want the job, I have to run Coach's plays perfectly."

She crossed her arms. "How come you take *his* advice but not mine?"

"Because *you* want me to wear yellow," I told

her. "And I'm a girl, not a banana." I held up my gym bag. "Now, if you'll excuse me, I have to lace up my turf talons."

I probably looked weird, clacking across the cafeteria's patio in my cleats while everyone else ate mini pizzas. And it was definitely tough running plays without anybody in the other positions, but I got it done and still managed to scarf down a burger before the bell rang. Never mind the fact that I probably smelled as bad as Sir Stinks a Lot.

Luckily, my Journalism teammates were too busy with their own issues to notice.

"I don't want to be middle ground!" Vanessa lamented again when we all sat in our group. "I want to be like Tim or Brooke. Loved or hated." She pointed to him, then to me.

"Thank you," I said.

"Listen, it's not all it's cracked up to be," said Tim. "My lunches are booked until next week, girls keep taking selfies with me, guys are telling me I'm hilarious. . . ."

Vanessa stared at him and drummed her fingers on the table. "Which of those was the bad part?"

"Oh, none," he said. "But I'm sure it's bound to happen."

"You picked a soft topic," I told Vanessa to distract her from choking him. "For something we thought was an exercise piece."

I emptied the contents of our advice box on the table. "Sort through these and find one that's bound to get people talking. And you"—I pointed to Heather—"don't really want another Gabby-style incident, do you?"

She breathed through her teeth. "No. Good point."

"Tim?"

"Keep on being awesome?"

I rolled my eyes. "No. You have to turn down

those lunch offers, because . . . rule number nine: We can't use our column for personal gain."

"Rule number nine?" said Tim. "What happened to rule number eight?"

"You're behind." I winked at the other girls as Tim took the rule book out of his backpack.

He looked to Vanessa, who filled him in, while Heather and I sorted advice. Even though I knew it wouldn't be in there, I still couldn't help looking for a sealed note just for me. Unfortunately, I was right, but Heather had quite a few requests waiting.

"Wow," she murmured, looking through them. "A lot of people need my help!"

Vanessa read over her shoulder. "Are there any having relationship problems *and* bad hair days?"

"You've got this one here." I pointed one out to Vanessa. "Is Velcro making a comeback?"

"No," she said. "There. All done with requests

for my help." She made a face.

"Aww, don't be like that, V," I said. "You're going to have weeks when everyone needs fashion advice. Like . . . Halloween."

She perked up a little. "Yeah, that'll be fun!"

We sorted advice until Mrs. H clapped her hands and Mary Patrick buzzed her brand-new buzzer.

"Staff meeting," said Mrs. H. "Everyone to the front."

There was a scraping of chairs and desks and a general jumble as everyone packed around the dry-erase board.

"Our first short issue is out of the way," said Mrs. H to a smattering of applause. "And our first full issue comes out next Monday, which means all columns are due on my desk *Friday*." She patted her in-basket for emphasis. "Before we get a progress report from each team, Mary Patrick has a few words."

Mrs. H stepped back, and Mary Patrick paced the floor.

"What day is today?" she asked.

"Mini-Pizza Day!" shouted Vanessa.

Several people laughed, and Heather whispered something into her ear.

"Uh . . . also Toughen-Up Tuesday!" Vanessa shouted again.

Mary Patrick pointed at her. "It's Toughen-Up Tuesday, when we get backlash from disgruntled readers and we get used to not *reacting* to it." She stared directly at me. "Or taking advantage of it." She shifted her gaze slightly to my left.

Tim shielded his eyes with a hand. "I feel warm. How red am I?" he whispered.

"I tooold you," I singsonged under my breath.

Mary Patrick decreed a few more toughen-up rules, no doubt directed at other mischief-makers, and then Mrs. H took progress updates from the different teams. Hearing that most people weren't very far along was reassuring . . . at least to me.

Mary Patrick's eyes lit with a little more fire each time someone said "almost." Every time a column was anything but complete, she reminded the writer that time was of the essence and good journalism waited for no one. For the most part, people grumbled and nodded. Stefan, however, had no problem defying Mary Patrick.

"I'll finish when I finish," he said. "If you want it now, it'll be sloppy, but if you wait, it'll be Pulitzer worthy."

Tim snorted. "I highly doubt that," he whispered.

"Be nice," said Heather. "Stefan's got talent."

"And you've got mushy crush brain," Tim countered.

But Mary Patrick didn't look like she believed in Stefan either. "Sure," she said. "And how are the photos coming for Meet the Faculty?"

"They'll be done in time too."

"Where are you on the list?" she pressed.

"Why does she keep picking on him?" mumbled Heather.

"I'm on *P*, as in 'pain in the butt,'" he said with a pointed expression.

Mary Patrick clenched her jaw and snorted air through her nostrils.

"Let's keep it civil," said Mrs. H. "Gil, how's the horoscope?"

"It's done," he said, "but I was also hoping to do an extra little feature on the thirteenth sign." He grinned at me. "Brooke inspired me."

Mrs. H nodded. "That would be perfect for the web edition, and thank you for the reminder!" She glanced around the room. "In addition to your current material, think of any little tidbits about your section that you might want to expand. Advice, for example, is going to respond to even more letters than in the paper edition."

She pointed to me. "How's that coming, by the way, Brooke?"

Three pairs of eyes were boring holes right through me.

I'd completely forgotten to tell my team about the website.

"Great!" I said without looking at them. "We're going through the letters right now."

"When do you think you'll be ready?" asked Mary Patrick.

"We'll finish when we finish," I told her.

Everyone laughed.

Shortly after, we broke back into small teams. I approached mine with my best please-don't-put-my-head-on-a-pike smile.

"Heeey, guys. There's something I need to tell you."

Tim stroked his chin. "Hmmm. Could it possibly be about the newspaper's website?"

I winced. "Sorry! I forgot to tell you because

that day we had the Meet the Press video."

"Which you also forgot to tell us about," said Vanessa.

"And how many extra responses do we have to come up with on short notice?" asked Heather.

I raised an eyebrow. I expected cattiness from Vanessa but never from sweet, sweet Heather. I countered with my own. "*You* wanted to help more people, remember?"

Heather sighed and twisted a piece of paper between her fingers. "I don't have a problem with helping," she said. "I have a problem with you getting info that affects the whole group and not passing it on."

"I second that," said Vanessa. "If I'd known about the video, I might not have frozen up."

"In my defense, I didn't see the email," I said.

"So check your emails," Tim said.

"In my defense, I forgot I'd be getting them," I said.

"So write a reminder," Heather said.

Everyone was being incredibly bossy today.

I took a deep breath. "We'll answer three additional letters each. And we'll do it right now in absolute silence."

Otherwise, I had a feeling chairs would soon be flying.

Nobody seemed to have a problem with that, so I grabbed my spiral notebook to get started on my own letters. A slip of paper fell out . . . my zodiac sign for the history project. I still hadn't researched all my topics.

"Darn it," I muttered, and got up to talk to Mrs. H.

"What can I do for you, Brooke?" she asked.

"I'd like to spend the rest of class in the library," I said. "Researching my advice responses."

Dear Lincoln's Letters, I'm a pathological liar. . . .

She nodded and handed me a hall pass. "I

think that's very professional."

I grabbed my books, and Heather, Vanessa, and Tim watched me.

"Where are you going?" asked Heather. "Are you upset because I yelled?"

I couldn't help smiling. "No, I'm going to the library. Are you even *capable* of yelling?"

"She's so musical, it probably comes out sounding like opera," said Vanessa, holding one hand to her chest and extending the other. "How dare you, *Brooooooooooke!*"

Heather laughed and clapped. "Bravo!"

"I'll see you guys later," I said.

Vanessa nudged Heather and Tim to mimic her.

"Good-byyyyyyyye!" she sang, and they joined in.

I rolled my eyes and hurried out of the room before they did an encore. I had twenty minutes before history class, so I sat at a computer and searched for my Mesopotamia topics. Normally, we were supposed to stick to reference books since anyone could post anything on the internet, but I figured I could get the info now and then find it in books later.

I jotted down all the info and even figured out how I'd feature each concept in the video. I should've felt better with the task out of my way, but I couldn't help thinking about everything else I had to do.

I still had to write the script for the history video, make the video, find (and answer) a great question for the column, do three others for the website, do the rest of my homework, make posters for my student council campaign, learn whatever new maneuvers Coach had shown the day I missed soccer, get a new uniform, and spend time with my friends and family.

Oh, and at some point I needed to sleep. And

bathe. I took a whiff of my shirt and wrinkled my nose.

The bell rang, and I gathered my stuff with the speed of a sloth. Maybe if I moved slower, time would slow down too. Heather was waiting for me in the hallway, twirling purple-tinted hair around her finger.

"Hey! How'd the research go?" she asked.

"Good!" I said. "And not even remotely related to the newspaper." I made a face. "I was a little behind on my history project."

"Ooh, that's my fault," she said. "I shouldn't have made us go to Vanessa's and spend so much time there."

"Yeah, but it was fun," I said.

"So fun!" she agreed with a smile. "And definitely not boring like someone said my advice was." She stuck out her tongue.

"Seriously? On the piece where you told

Finders Keepers to give the wallet back?"

She nodded and pulled a slip of paper from her pocket. "Apparently, the correct response was 'Use the money to buy a dwarf rabbit. Ike Gillespie's birthday is coming up.'"

"Gee, I wonder who wrote *that* note."

Heather laughed. "Anyway, I wanted to say sorry for how I acted earlier. You've got a lot going on, and it's easy to forget the little stuff."

"I'm sorry too," I said. "The start of school has been hectic, but I shouldn't let my life affect you guys."

"And I wanted to offer to take care of compiling our web content," she said. "Gil came by when you were gone and started asking a bunch of formatting questions. I told him I'd handle it, but I wanted to make sure you were okay with that."

I wasn't sure how to respond. On one hand, I shouldn't have needed someone else to bail me out. But on the other hand, I hadn't even thought about what we'd need to do for the website.

"Brooke?"

"You . . . are my favorite person today," I finally told Heather, giving her a big hug. "How can I repay you? Would you like a pony?"

She laughed again. "You can afford a pony?"

"A miniature one," I said, almost touching the tips of my thumb and index fingers together. "Like . . . this big."

"How about you just get me your three web pieces by Friday? Oh!" She reached into her other pocket. "And to make it easier, Vanessa, Tim, and I already picked your questions for you."

"The three of you will have to share the pony," I told her, taking the paper. "You don't each get one."

"I don't need a pony. Just one happy Brooke," she said with a smile.

CHAPTER

9

Van Jackson

I was on the edge of the soccer field, lacing my cleats, when someone bumped into my back, almost knocking me down.

"Oh no! Sorry, Number Three!" Lacey clapped a hand to her cheek in mock sympathy. "I couldn't see you from all the way up here in the number-two spot!"

So she'd heard about my ranking.

"I wouldn't brag about being number two!" I shouted after her, but she was already halfway across the field. It wasn't my best comeback, anyway.

I gave my laces a test tug and straightened up, jogging over to Coach.

"Jacobs!" he said. "You're back to your natural color."

"Yes, sir. I'm back, I'm bad, and I'm better than ever." I posed with my hands on my hips.

"Is that so?" he asked, opening a bag of soccer balls and dumping them onto the grass. "Planning to take over the number-one spot?"

I hooked my foot under a ball and popped it into the air. "I've got a few tricks up my sleeve."

I had zero tricks up my sleeve. Or down my sock. Or in my ear. The only thing I could do was take Coach's advice and try running his plays.

The only problem? They'd learned a new one while I was out the day before.

While the other girls carried the balls on to the field to practice, Coach showed me a diagram of his latest play, called "Screaming Meanie." And I asked roughly five thousand questions.

"I promise you're making it harder than it needs to be," he said. "Just follow along and learn as you go."

No practice runs? Wonderful.

He blew the whistle and everyone hustled into position. The ball was kicked into play and . . . I might as well have been dancing *The Nutcracker*.

I tried to remember everything Coach had shown me, but with all the motion and yelling, it was hard enough to keep up with the ball. I didn't want to get deductions for doing my own thing, but I couldn't just stand there, so I ran.

"Wrong way, Number Three!" Lacey shouted at me.

I pivoted on one foot and took off in the opposite direction. I started to realize something might be amiss when the only thing around me was a bird nibbling grass seeds.

Lacey had sent me in the opposite direction of the action.

"Jacobs, what are you doing?" called Coach. "Quit picking flowers and get over here!"

Hanging my head in embarrassment, I charged back across the field just in time to see Lacey score a point. Her teammates cheered, and she smirked in my direction.

Luckily, I'm a fast learner, so when the next group ran the play, I watched the girl in my position and compared it to the sheet on Coach's clipboard. The second time I ran that play? Lacey was eating *my* grass clippings.

"Better," Coach told me at the end of practice. "Much better."

I didn't bother pointing out that I'd scored zero goals with this new system.

"You look like you could use a sundae," Mom said when she picked me up. "Let's get some ice cream and bananas and chocolate syrup."

"And an orange," I told her. "And some poster board and glitter, please."

Mom wrinkled her nose. "I think they're going to taste terrible together, but okay."

I laughed. "The orange is for a mystery I'm trying to solve, and the poster board and glitter are to make campaign signs. I'm running for sixth-grade president."

"That's wonderful!" said Mom. "What's your platform?"

"My what?"

"Your political platform. Where do you stand on the issues?"

"Uh . . ." I stared ahead. "No on homework, yes on lunches?"

She smiled. "I mean the issues that the kids at your school complain about. What are the big problems?"

I didn't answer.

"It's something you should consider," she said. "And it tells people why they should vote for you instead of a different candidate."

We grabbed a cart at the store and ran into our neighbor Miss Lillian.

"Nikki and Brooke, so nice to see you both!" she said, beaming. "I actually had a favor to ask of Brooke. I completely forgot about a meeting I have Thursday night and could really use someone to watch Rocket for a few hours. Would you be free after six?"

Rocket was Miss Lillian's award-winning terrier.

I nodded. "Sure. Soccer practice will be over by then."

"Perfect!" She waggled her fingers at us. "I'm off to ask the butcher for a ham bone. That's all Rocket will eat, you know. Fussy little thing."

Mom and I smiled at each other, then returned to our shopping.

"I'm surprised you have time to help with all that you've got going on," she said.

"I'll manage," I said. "This ice cream will give me strength."

It gave me brain freeze.

After enjoying a big bowlful, I set to work reading through the advice requests my friends had picked for me, looking for the perfect one for the paper. Most of them I skimmed, but one of them caught my eye.

Dear Lincoln's Letters,

I know this doesn't fall into any of your categories, but I don't know what to do, so here goes. Middle school is killing me. I'm so swamped with activities that I don't know where to start. I don't have time for my friends, and all the things I love to do seem like work instead of fun. The worst part? The school year just started! What do I do?

Overwhelmed and Miserable

I could have written this letter. I know I'd told Mom that I was going to pull it all together, but I also had no idea how I was going to do it. I wanted to give advice to Overwhelmed and Miserable, but how could I possibly tell someone how to handle it all when I didn't even know?

I pinned the letter on the bulletin board and stared at it. Then I shifted my gaze to the one beside it for Young Sherlocks.

A girl is missing from her classroom. Someone has left an orange peel on her notebook. What now?

I peeled the orange, ate the fleshy parts, and set the peel on my desk. Then I waited.

Nothing happened.

I didn't disappear; no answer magically revealed itself. My entire room simply smelled like citrus.

"Why are you so important?" I mumbled to the peel before pinning it on my bulletin board too. So far I was making great progress in all my endeavors.

I shifted to thinking about student council. What was something that I'd heard kids complain about? The food, the smell in the gym . . . Could I do something about either of those? Overwhelmed and Miserable was complaining about not having enough time.

I set to work on my poster, making sure to pour on the glitter. People liked shiny, sparkly things.

VOTE BROOKE JACOBS FOR SIXTH-GRADE PRESIDENT
A vote for Brooke means . . .
Better food!
No more smelly gym!
More time to get things done!

If I could give students more time to get things done, that would benefit me too. A win-win situation! Satisfied, I started the rest of my homework.

The next morning, I hopped out of Mom's car with my glitter-trailing poster and waited for Vanessa at our usual spot by the fountain. A girl I didn't recognize approached me.

"Are you waiting for Vanessa?"

"Uh . . . yeah," I told her.

"Cool." The girl pulled out a book and started reading.

Another girl walked over.

"Are you guys waiting for Vanessa?"

The girl with the book nodded. "We're the start of the line."

"Awesome." The second girl stood next to the first and pulled out her phone.

I regarded both of them with a stare.

"Sorry, but what's going on here?"

The girl with the book looked at me as if I'd asked what planet we were on. "We're waiting for Vanessa."

"Right, I got that. I know why *I'm* waiting for Vanessa," I said. "But why are you?"

"For the same reason you are," said the other girl, wrinkling her forehead. "Free beauty profiles."

I sighed and stared at the sky. "Oh, V."

"What's your poster?" the girl with the book asked while three more girls joined our line.

I opened it so she could read. "I'm running for sixth-grade president," I said. "Are you a sixth grader?"

She nodded and scanned the poster. "What kind of food?"

"Sorry?"

She pointed to the line. "You say 'better food.'

What kind? Tofu?"

I snorted. "That's not better. That's gross . . . ly underappreciated," I finished after seeing the look on her face. "But I meant thick, juicy burgers that take more than two bites to eat and nachos with melty cheese sauce, not cold cheese slices."

"Yum!" said another girl. "You've got my vote!"

"And no more gym?" said another. "I'm totally onboard!"

I glanced down at my sign. "No, there's still gym. It just won't be as smelly."

"Single file, please, ladies!" Tim strolled over, sporting dark sunglasses. "You'll all get your—" He froze when he saw the expression on my face. "Uh-oh."

"Tim? You're part of this madness?" I gestured at the line.

Tim took off his shades, and a chorus of excited whispers went up. "Man! I told Vanessa you wouldn't like it."

"Hey, Shakespeare!" one of the girls said with a nervous giggle.

"Will you sign my copy of the *Lincoln Log?*" asked another. "Don't forget to include your phone number."

The whole line dissolved into giggles.

Tim gave them all a wave and then turned to me. "So you're here for a beauty consultation?"

"Don't try to distract me," I said. "Why are you guys doing this?"

"Vanessa was feeling bad about her Meet the Press video, so when she suggested this, Heather and I thought—"

I clapped my hand to my forehead. "Heather's in on this too?"

Tim's eyes widened, and he glanced around for an escape. "So you're getting rid of gym!" He pointed to my sign.

"The *smell*," I said. "I'm getting rid of smelly gym. And quit changing the subject! Where's Heather?"

"Right there," he said, pointing past me and slipping his shades back on. "Ladies"—he addressed the line—"the makeover master has arrived."

"Yaaaay!" They all cheered as Vanessa approached, Heather walking a step behind her with a black cosmetic case and folding chair.

I didn't share the group's enthusiasm. "Oh. *No*."

Vanessa was wearing huge sunglasses and a black trench coat, a shiny red bag slung over one shoulder. She said something to Heather and waved the fingertips of one hand at the girls in line. When she realized I was among them, she momentarily paused, with Heather nearly colliding into her, sunglasses falling askew. After a beat, she regained her stride.

"Brooke, sweetheart, how *are* you?" she asked in a snooty voice.

"I'm sane, thanks! How are you?" I leaned in closer to her and Heather. "And more important, what the heck are you two doing?"

"Increasing my fan base, darling. It's all the rage these days." She perched on the edge of the fountain and let her red bag slide down beside her. "Heather, dear! The chair."

Heather smiled apologetically at me and set up the folding chair to face Vanessa. Tim stood with one hand on his hip and the other hand out, holding back the line.

"It's all right, Timothy." Vanessa made a beckoning gesture. "You may let the first girl through. Heather, would you be a love and fetch me a Frappuccino?"

"Um . . . I don't think the cafeteria sells those," said Heather. "How about chocolate milk?"

"With a straw, please?" asked Vanessa. "Have the lunch lady charge it to my account. And get yourself a little something, too." She winked at Heather.

Heather nodded and turned to me. "Do you want—" My scowl deepened. "Never mind. I'll be right back!" She trotted away.

I ran my fingers through my hair. "V—"

"It's Van Jackson, darling. Van Jackson," cooed Vanessa. "And don't crinkle your hair like that. Crimping is so five seasons ago."

"Excuse me." The girl with the book tapped my shoulder. "If you're not going to get a consultation, can I go?"

"Wh-Wha . . . B-bu . . ." All I could do was sputter as I stepped aside.

"Now, sweetie, what's your name?" Vanessa asked the girl, pulling a magnifying glass out of her makeup case.

"Uh . . . Charity," she said. Her eyes followed Vanessa's magnifying glass as it swooped closer to her face.

Vanessa's mouth appeared huge in the lens. "Your pores are so perfect and tiny, Charity!"

She beamed. "Thanks! I was actually hoping you could show me how to apply blush."

"Of course!" Vanessa reached into her makeup case and pulled out an entire tray filled with blushes.

"Whoa," said Tim, who'd turned around for a second to watch. "You wear all those?"

"For different occasions," said Vanessa, pointing to each one. "This is for summer, and this is for winter, and this is for formal occasions, and this . . ."

She was having to talk louder and louder as the girls in line began to press toward her, ignoring Tim's hand of justice.

"What is she doing?" someone asked.

"I can't see!" cried someone else.

"One at a time!" called Tim. But his looks and charm apparently couldn't keep a throng of girls from slowly pushing him to the side so they could surround Vanessa and the poor girl in the chair, who was now using her book as a shield.

"Can I try the winter blush?" A girl made a swipe for Vanessa's makeup case.

"Okay," said Tim, grabbing my arm and holding out a hand for Vanessa. "This is about to get dangerous."

"Nonsense!" said Vanessa, waving around a makeup palette as she spoke. "It's—"

"Ooh, MAC!" Someone nabbed the palette, almost taking V's hand with it.

"Okay, let's go." Vanessa got up, pulling Charity with her. Instantly, the other girls pounced on the makeup case. In the chaos, someone crashed into me and knocked the poster out of my hand. I bent down to get it, but Tim pulled me back.

"Leave it," he said. "There's no time!"

"But I put a whole five minutes into that," I protested as he dragged me and Vanessa toward the school. Heather met us on her way out, holding a bottle of chocolate milk and a package of powdered doughnuts.

"What are you guys doing over here?" She squinted at the cluster around the fountain. "And why are there three girls fighting over an eyelash curler?"

"Right? You'd think they'd never seen quality beauty products before," said Vanessa.

"The beauty consultation got a little out of hand," I explained to Heather.

Tim nodded. "When it's over, all that's going to be left is the skeleton of V's makeup case."

She sighed. "Well, at least I know what I'm asking for at Christmas."

"Sorry, V." Heather held out the bottle of chocolate milk.

"Ohhh, not as sorry as she's going to be." Tim cocked his head ever so slightly toward the archway in front of the building.

Mary Patrick stood beneath it, surveying the chaos. Slowly, her head swiveled until she was looking at us.

"Make that 'Not as sorry as we're all going to be,'" I amended.

CHAPTER

10

Advice from the Hart

"Sit," said Mrs. H, pointing to our desks in the Journalism room. "And explain those ridiculous getups." Her frown was so deep, the corners of her mouth were practically touching her chin. Mary Patrick stood next to her with a similar look of disdain.

"Um . . . we're method acting?" suggested Tim, taking a seat.

"*I'm* not wearing a ridiculous getup," I said, sitting on top of my desk.

Mary Patrick arched a brow. "Your entire

outfit and face are covered in gold. You look like an Academy Award."

I glanced down at my glitter-coated T-shirt.

The campaign poster.

"Well, that was an accident," I said, swiping my hands over my face and plucking at my shirt to free the glitter. "It came from a campaign poster I made."

"And you three, the dark sunglasses crew?" Mary Patrick pointed at Heather, Vanessa, and Tim.

"They were helping me," Vanessa said in her normal voice. She blushed. "I was a beauty consultant."

"You almost started a riot," Mary Patrick informed her. "There are three teachers outside—"

"Thank you, Mary Patrick," interrupted Mrs. H, placing a hand on her shoulder. "I think I can handle this."

Mary Patrick nodded but continued to glare at us.

Vanessa fidgeted in her chair. "Mrs. H, I'm sorry. I just wanted the other kids to know that I'm a good advice columnist."

"And we just wanted to support her," said Heather. "You know . . . as a team."

Mrs. H relaxed her scowl. "Vanessa, nobody has said you're not a good advice columnist. Have they?" She turned to Mary Patrick, who shook her head almost reluctantly. "If you want people to be confident in your answers, you have to be confident in yourself."

Vanessa bowed her head. "Yes, ma'am."

"Heather and Tim." Mrs. H crossed her arms. "It's admirable that you want to support your friend, but not when your support fuels unhealthy behavior. This is your chance to put your skills to good use and help her make a better choice, not enable a bad one."

Heather's eyes filled with tears. "I'm an enabler?" she whispered.

Tim, for once, didn't have a snappy comeback.

"And Brooke." Mrs. H shifted her gaze to me.

"I know. Less glitter on the posters," I said, brushing off my sleeve.

"No, you're the section lead. You should be aware of what your columnists are doing and how they're feeling."

I gawked at her. "But they did this behind my back!"

"Because they didn't feel they could talk to you about it," said Mrs. H. "And that's a problem. They should always be coming to you first if they have issues regarding the column." She looked from Vanessa to Heather to Tim. "True?"

They all mumbled their agreement.

I pressed my lips together but didn't say

anything further. Mary Patrick took advantage of the moment's silence to blurt what had been on her mind.

"You four need to decide if you're writing this advice column to help other people or to help yourselves. Do you even care about the students who are writing to you?"

Mrs. H raised an eyebrow. "That's enough, Mary Patrick. I think they understand." She glanced at the clock on the wall. "The bell's about to ring for homeroom, so you're free to go, but I expect better from all of you in the future."

The four of us got to our feet and shuffled out the door. When we got to the hall, Vanessa turned to the rest of us, twisting her hands together while she spoke.

"I'm sorry, you guys. I didn't mean to get you in trouble." She turned and walked off without another word.

"V, wait!" Heather chased after her, and

Tim frowned at me.

"I told you I wasn't right for this job," he said, sauntering away.

I slid to the floor next to the advice box. "Fantastic."

Abel walked toward me, stuffing his hands into his pockets.

"Please, just keep moving," I said.

"Are you waiting for someone to drop a note in the advice box?" he asked. "Or offering a drive-through version of your services?" He cupped a hand over his mouth. "Welcome to Advice in the Box. May I take your issue?"

I couldn't help smiling. "Neither. In fact, if you listen to Mary Patrick, that box shouldn't even be on the wall." I glanced up at it. "She says my friends and I don't care about other people."

Instead of laughing in my face or making a snide remark, Abel just stood there. "Why would she say that?"

For once, he didn't seem to be teasing me, so I explained what happened in the courtyard and the fallout from it.

"And you're just going to let someone else tell you who you are?" Abel scoffed. "That's pretty weak, Brooke. I thought you were different."

Something tingled in the back of my mind. "What did you say?"

"I said 'that's pretty weak,'" Abel repeated. "To let Mary Patrick's opinion affect you."

"She's the editor of the paper," I pointed out.

"That doesn't mean she's right," said Abel. "You're still interested in Young Sherlocks, aren't you?"

I nodded and sighed. "I know the deadline is coming up. I'm still trying to figure out the mystery."

"That's not what I'm getting at," said Abel. "A good detective uses research, evidence, and intuition to draw conclusions. Do you think Mary Patrick did any research to prove you and your friends don't care about other kids?"

I laughed. "Of course not."

"If she didn't do research, she can't possibly have evidence, and she's relying strictly on intuition. And believe me, that's not saying much." Abel leaned forward confidentially. I could smell a mixture of cologne and French fries on him. It was oddly . . . nice.

"What, she's not superintuitive?" I asked with a smile.

"Last year, when a strange photo appeared in her locker, Mary Patrick was convinced someone was trying to send her a secret message," said Abel. "The photo actually belonged to the owner of the locker above her. It had simply slipped through the cracks,"

I snorted. "I see your point."

The bell rang, and I got to my feet.

"I've gotta go, but thanks for the pep talk," I told him. "I honestly didn't expect it from you."

He shrugged but turned pink. "I pick on you a lot, and if you want to join Young Sherlocks, it would probably be good for us to get along. Anyway, I hope I helped."

I nodded. "More than you know. I'll talk to you later." I waved good-bye, but instead of going to my homeroom, I headed to a different one.

When Tim saw me walk into the room, he stiffened. "Uh-oh. What'd I do now?"

"I'm not here to see you," I told him. "I'm here to see Gabby." I turned to his sister. "Hi!"

"Hey, Brooke! Did you want to talk about our history project?" she asked. "Listen, I know you wanted to work on the script, but I was so excited I came up with a little something myself. It's in my locker."

First Heather was handling the website, and now Gabby was handling the history project?

I forced a smile. "That's perfect! I know how much you love history, so you probably did a better job than I could've done. But I actually came to talk to you about something else." I crouched next to her desk. "You said you came up with an idea after that mess with Jefferson. What was it?"

Even though I ended up being late to homeroom, it was worth it to hear Gabby's explanation. At lunchtime I headed outside and ran soccer plays while I thought about who my friends were at their very centers. Abel had been right; Mary Patrick didn't know a thing about us.

At the start of Journalism, Heather and Vanessa were sitting at their desks, lost in their own worlds as they scribbled in their notebooks. Heather wrote song lyrics, and Vanessa sketched outfits. Tim and I walked in together, with Gabby right behind us.

"Hey, guys!" I greeted Heather and Vanessa. "I brought a special guest."

They looked up and smiled when they saw Gabby.

"Hey!" Vanessa waved her fuzzy pencil topper.

"How's it going?" asked Heather, getting up to hug Gabby. "I haven't seen you around the halls."

"I'm good!" said Gabby. "I've just been really busy with my new project."

I cleared my throat. "A new project inspired by the members of this advice column," I said, gesturing to all of us.

"Really?" Vanessa put down her notebook.

Gabby nodded. "I was so lucky to have you guys help me through the situation with Jefferson, and I realized not every girl has friends like that. So I took your advice and did something productive with the situation."

I held up my phone so they could see the picture I'd taken. It was the outside of a locker with a badge numbered 411.

"You changed lockers?" guessed Heather.

"Well, yes," said Gabby. "But I also created this." She pointed at me, and I swiped to the next picture of the locker's interior, filled with binders on less-than-typical school subjects.

"Dating, friendship, parents . . . ," Vanessa read, smiling. "What is this?"

"It's Locker 411," said Gabby. "My mom helped me come up with the name, because 411 was the slang for information when she was a kid. Basically, it'll have all the information a girl could want to survive middle school." She smiled mischievously. "I may have even included a warning about a certain rat-weasel of a guy from a different school. And anyone can access the information because I rigged the lock on the door handle."

"That's ingenious!" said Heather, reaching for my phone so she could get a closer look.

I stopped her. "Heather, you did the right

thing this morning."

She blinked up at me. "What? No."

"Vanessa was going to pull her Van Jackson routine whether you tried to talk her out of it or not," I said, looking to V for support.

She nodded. "It's true. When I get something in my head, I have to go through with it."

"You and Tim being there to support her probably kept it from being much worse than it did." I cleared my throat. "Regardless of the mini-riot."

"But shouldn't we have stopped her like we stopped Gabby?" asked Heather.

I shook my head. "Gabby was different. She was trying to hurt someone, not help them." I smiled apologetically at her. "Sorry."

Gabby waved a dismissive hand. "You're not wrong."

"My point is," I said, "V's actions weren't going to hurt anyone, and the fact that she went to such great lengths to prove she could help people just shows how much she *wants* to help. And what we did for Gabby inspired her to do something for even more people."

"I know I'm the last person who should be talking," chimed in Tim, "but Mary Patrick is wrong. We spend every class going through advice requests and trying to answer them the best we can because we do care."

Heather's lower lip trembled, but she nodded firmly, a fierce glow in her eyes.

"Heck yes, we do!" cried Vanessa. "I care so much I sacrificed an entire case of makeup!"

Heather, Gabby, Tim, and I laughed.

"Hey, I should go to my own class," said Gabby, "but if you guys wouldn't mind talking up Locker 411 to whoever you can, I'd appreciate it!"

"It's the least we can do since you boosted our spirits," I said, waving as she headed for the door.

Especially when a minute later Mrs. H gave a long lecture on ethics. She avoided looking at my team directly, but we knew what prompted it. We also knew we were good at what we did. Nevertheless, during small-group time I had Tim write three new rules in the book:

Rule #10: believe in your answers and yourself.

Rule #11: practice what you preach.

Rule #12: don't take your problems out on others.

Heather also reminded us that she still needed everyone's pieces for the website, though her gaze fell on Tim and me.

"I'll get it to you tonight," he promised.

"Mine will be tomorrow," I said. "I'm dog-sitting for Miss Lillian then, so I'll have plenty of time to work on it."

In history, Gabby presented the script she'd created, and Spencer complimented her on how good it was. She blushed and beamed, and I knew Jefferson was a thing of the past.

I had to admit Gabby's script was pretty entertaining *and* educational, and when we met that night at Spencer's house to film with all our artifacts, the whole thing really came together.

"This is gonna be great!" said Gabby when we were finished.

"I'll add voice-over to this," I said, taking the flash drive out of the camera. "And some on-screen text to go with our scenes."

"Perfect!" said Ashley.

I made it home with just enough light outside to run thirty minutes of practice plays, incorporating a few of my own steps. If I was going to be forced to do things how Coach wanted, I needed to find a way to make those goals.

Dad came out to call me in for dinner, and I got to show him.

"Not bad!" he said. "You'll give your teammates

a run for their money. I wish I could be there to see it."

"I wish you could too," I said with a frown. "Do you really have to work late so much?"

"Honey, when you get to be my age . . . in a thousand years," he said with a wink, "you'll realize that your priorities change. Providing for my family comes before everything else."

"Yeah, but even then before your own family?" I asked.

Dad sighed and kissed the top of my head. "It's hard to explain, but what I'm doing *is* putting my family first."

"Okay," I said, rolling the ball between my hands.

"But I've got some free time tonight!" he said, taking the ball from me. "We could watch a match I recorded after dinner if you're not busy."

A flurry of tasks flew through my brain, and I disregarded them all. Family first, right?

"Nope! I'm all caught up!"

Over dinner we were able to convince Mom to join us *and* make kettle corn, the perfect combination for a fun family evening. The next morning, however, I was up before the sun to do my narration for the history video.

Honestly? I'd never added audio to a video before, but the online instructions seemed pretty simple, so I uploaded the video and did a sample recording. After a few practices, it sounded great and synced up perfectly. I replaced the file, threw the flash drive into my bag, and picked up Hammie, who had been licking my desk.

"What are you eating?" I asked. "There's nothing there."

She mewed and went back to licking.

Cats. Such a simple, perfect life.

I caught up with Vanessa outside of school, where she'd traded her sunglasses and trench coat for her usual cutting-edge fashion. Today's was a skirt made from strips of colored duct tape woven together.

"Whoa!" I said. "How long did that take you?"

"Only a couple weeks. The tricky part was getting the tape off my eyebrows."

"How . . ."

"Long story. How did your history video go?"

"Great!" I said. "Want to see? We do all our own stunts."

Her eyes widened. "Ooh. Running from giant boulders and jumping across rooftops?"

"Yes," I said. "If by giant boulders you mean bees and by rooftops you mean blades of grass."

"Sounds riveting," she said. "I'm in!"

We went to the computer lab, and I plugged in the flash drive.

"Prepare to be dazzled!" I said. And then my voice came through the speakers.

But the screen stayed dark.

"What was it like to be an ancient

Mesopotamian?" Voice-Over Me said.

"Ooh. Spooky lead-in," said Vanessa.

"It's not supposed to be dark like that. There should be video by now," I said while Voice-Over Me kept talking.

I closed the file and reopened it.

"What was it like to be an ancient Mesopotamian?"

"No, no, no." I closed the file and opened the flash drive's home folder. The only thing in it was my recording. I opened it and dragged the cursor halfway through the recording. ". . . enjoyed a hearty meal of barley . . ."

I clutched Vanessa's arm and whispered, "V. The video's gone. They're going to kill me."

"Well, hang on." She tapped her chin thoughtfully. "Can you tell people the Mesopotamians were blind?"

"No."

"That the sun didn't exist back then?"

"No."

"Do you have another copy of the video?"

"No."

She clicked her tongue. "Yeah, they're gonna kill you."

I dropped my face onto the keyboard, which beeped in dismay.

"If you want, I can go with you when you tell them," she said. "Then you guys can refilm it today."

I shook my head. "They all have stuff to do. I'm going to have to remake it myself and make it even better."

"Then do you want help with *that*?" she asked.

"No, it's fine. Since it'll be just me, it'll be quick to film, anyway. I'll do it at Miss Lillian's tonight."

"I thought you were going to do your website advice tonight," Vanessa reminded me.

I made a face. "Shoot! Well, I'll do that in class today."

And when Journalism rolled around, I started to write to Overwhelmed and Miserable . . . until Tim dropped into the seat beside me.

"I'm stuck," he said.

"Stuck? Did you sit in gum?" I craned my neck to look at his chair.

"Not literally! I've got writer's block." He scratched his head with both hands. "People really liked my first piece, and now I feel like I have to keep up that momentum but . . . I'm stuck!"

I sighed and pushed my notebook aside. "Okay, which letter did you pick?"

He held up a slip of paper.

> Dear Lincoln's Letters,
> How do I get a girl to notice me?
> Invisible Boy

Tim then referred to his notebook. "So I wrote, 'Dear Invisible Boy.'" He glanced up. "That's all I've got."

"You get girls to notice you all the time!" I said. "You should have plenty of suggestions."

"Yeah, but it's hit or miss what works. Sometimes I act British and girls think it's charming. Other times they run away before I even twirl my cane."

I curled my lip. "I'm surprised all of them don't hit you with it."

"In his defense, canes are making a comeback among the avant-garde," said Vanessa.

"What are those?" I asked. "Old people?"

Heather put a hand on my arm to stop me from talking. "Tim, other than the cane, how do you get girls to notice you?"

"I don't know. It's not like I keep a list so I can use it again," he said. Then he rubbed his chin. "Although that's not a bad idea."

"It's easy to get someone to notice you," said Vanessa. "Just do something weird. Like wear a plaid suit."

"I think Invisible Boy wants the girl to notice him in a good way, V," said Heather. "That would send me running."

Vanessa smirked. "Yeah, okay. But if we saw a kid show up to school in a plaid suit, we'd know who Invisible Boy was."

"Listen, here's the best advice," I told Tim, who was looking even more confused. "Tell him to find out what the girl he likes is interested in. Then he can do things around those interests to get her to notice him."

Tim started to write.

"Like, if she's into bears, he could dress up as a bear," said Vanessa.

I rolled my eyes. "Nobody needs to dress up as anything. Just have him learn about her interests."

"And be confident," said Heather. "And smile. Girls like that."

"And he could write her notes," I said. "As long as she knows they're from him. And he doesn't stop sending them."

Heather made a sympathetic sound. "Still nothing from the secret admirer?"

I shook my head. "Oh well. Like Tim said, maybe he wasn't someone I'd be interested in, anyway. He probably twirled a cane."

Tim launched his pen at me while Heather and Vanessa laughed. We talked through his letter and response, occasionally interjecting on what we thought might be funny. Before I knew it, class was over and I was walking with Heather to history. And I hadn't worked on a single piece of my advice.

"Hey, Brooke! Did you bring our video?" asked Spencer, catching up to us.

"I . . . actually left it at home to make a few

last-minute tweaks," I said. "But I'll definitely have it here tomorrow!"

"Cool," he said. He glanced around and ever so casually asked, "How's your campaign for sixth-grade president coming?"

"I think we both know it isn't," I said.

"Cool," he said again with a smile. "I might win this one."

"You thought Brooke was a threat?" asked Heather.

"Don't sound like it's impossible!" I bumped her. "I've got some pretty great ideas."

"Yeah, I heard about your better lunches and canceling gym," he said. "With that and your connections to the paper, I wouldn't be able to compete. Especially not with Dane Meiser running too." He waved. "Well, see ya in class."

Mr. Costas showed us a History Channel video on earlier civilizations to get us amped up to turn in our own videos. I tried to pay attention to the footage so I could improve my remake. But at the same time I couldn't stop watching Spencer, who was clearly not paying attention to the video either. Instead, he was looking at notecards on his desk and reading them quietly to himself, occasionally glancing at a pretend audience.

Was he practicing a campaign speech? Did that mean I had to write one too? Geez, running for president was a lot of work! But Spencer didn't look like he minded. He was as focused on getting that position as I was on getting team captain for the Strikers.

At least Coach was noticing my effort. That afternoon at practice, I ran every play exactly like he called it and earned a "Good form, Jacobs!"

"Too bad it's too little too late," Lacey said under her breath. "You can't suddenly pretend to play by the rules. It's obvious what you're doing. Butt kisser."

"I am not!"

"The worst part? You're not even getting any goals. What kind of leader are you?" She cackled and trotted off with one of her friends.

"Hey!" I chased after her. "Being a good leader isn't about making all the goals! Sometimes it's about letting someone else get the point while you get the assist. And being a good sport and not laughing at people when they fall down!"

Lacey snorted. "Thanks for that advice. I'll remember it when I'm team captain."

Every time I kicked the ball after that I imagined Lacey's head. Especially when the prize tickets for the first Chicago Fire game went to her.

CHAPTER

11

Rocket Launch

A couple hours later I was knocking on Miss Lillian's door. She greeted me with a hug while Rocket leaped halfway up my body using his tiny legs.

Even though he moves like he has jet-powered paws, Rocket was named for the shape of his nose. He's a purebred bull terrier.

"Careful that he doesn't try to climb all the way over your shoulder," Miss Lillian said with a chuckle. "He's still fond of his obstacle course days."

"Obstacle course?" I asked. "I thought he was a show dog."

"He started by running courses as a pup," she said. "When he got a little older, I shifted him over to the shows."

I followed her into the kitchen, where Rocket wagged his tail so hard, it thumped against the cupboard doors.

"Geez, he's got energy everywhere," I said, bending down to scratch behind his ears.

Miss Lillian slid her purse onto her shoulder. "Okay, Brooke, I'll be back in a few hours. You're welcome to whatever's in the pantry or refrigerator, though it's mainly Rocket's ham bones." She chuckled again. "If he gets too rowdy, just throw him one and he won't make a peep."

"Thanks for the advice," I said. "Have a fun evening!"

I scratched Rocket behind the ears again. "How would you like to be a movie star?"

It was a brilliant idea, if I did say so myself. People loved cute animals doing cute things, so

I'd just have Rocket be the main actor for my history project. And I'd call my video *MesoPET-amia*.

First on the script was a feast. I dug through the pantry and found some pita bread and dried apricots, and I dumped a can of vegetable stew into an earthenware bowl. I had Rocket sit in the backyard with the food spread before him and stepped back to film him with my phone.

"Something's missing," I said.

Rocket tilted his head to one side and yawned, curling out his tongue.

"A shelter!" I said, snapping my fingers.

Miss Lillian had a pile of scrap wood stacked beside her shed, including some old fence boards.

I angled them against the shed's wall and then studied the end result.

"It sure looks like primitive people made it," I said.

The doorbell rang, and Rocket barked,

zooming toward the house. I trotted after him and peeked through the front door's peephole. Heather was on the other side.

I picked up Rocket before he could paw a hole through the wood, and opened the door.

"Hi! What are you doing here?" I asked, giving Heather a hug.

"I just came to see if you needed any help with your advice for the website," she said. "Hi, Rocket!"

He wriggled in my arms and licked Heather's hand.

"Um . . . I actually haven't started yet. I need to film my video for history first."

Heather frowned. "I thought you guys did that yesterday."

"We did. And then I messed it up in editing," I said with a sheepish look. "So I'm redoing it now. I've already set up the feast and shelter! Come on, I'll show you."

She followed me out to the backyard, where I pointed out my work.

"Ta-da!"

"Nice feast!" she said. "Where's the shelter?"

I pointed at the boards. "Right here."

She cocked her head. "Ohhh. Sorry. The rake handle sticking out from the side threw me off."

"It's not much," I said, "but it'll protect Rocket from the elements." I patted one of the boards.

It shifted and fell over.

"Whoops!" I lowered Rocket to the ground and bent to pick up the board, placing it carefully among the others. "Okay, Rocket, you ready for the feast?" I patted the grass behind the spread.

Rocket sniffed at the different items and flopped onto one side.

"Come on, Rocket!" I coaxed. "Apricots. Yum!" I picked one up and pushed it against his mouth. He sneezed all over my hand. "Yuck!"

"Maybe he'd like some stew," tried Heather, bringing the bowl closer. "Look, Rocket!" She leaned down and took a deep whiff. Then she made a face. "Ugh! What's in this? It smells like dog food!"

"If it was, Rocket would eat it," I said.

Heather put the bowl down. "Why don't you just bring out some dog food, then?"

"It wouldn't be historically accurate," I said.

She gave me a dubious look. "I think history went out the window when you cast a dog to play a Mesopotamian."

I got to my feet. "Good point. I'll be right back."

I went into the kitchen, with Rocket on my heels, and grabbed one of his ham bones out of the refrigerator. At the sight of it, his tail went wild, and he ran right alongside me back to the yard, leaping to get at the bone. Since he wasn't used to having the woodpile spread out so far, he ran straight into it, and several boards jostled free and toppled sideways.

"Look out!" I cried.

Heather glanced up and quickly curled into a ball. I winced as one of the boards crashed down hard on her hand.

"Ow!" she yelped.

I dropped Rocket's bone and hurried to help Heather. "Are you okay? How's your hand?"

"It stings," she said, sitting up and rubbing at the scratches.

"Wait," I said. "Don't do that. Let's clean it first to make sure it doesn't get infected."

I led her inside to the bathroom and pulled out a first-aid kit while she cleaned her wounds.

"It's really not so bad," she said. "I don't think I need all that."

"I'm sorry," I said. "I didn't know Rocket was going to get so excited."

"It's okay," she said, showing me her scratched

hand. "See? No blood. Let's go rebuild your shelter and film Rocket."

"Good idea," I said, leading the way outside. "I hope he didn't get hurt when the boards fell. Rocket?"

No blur of fur approached me.

"Rocket?" I walked behind the shed, but he wasn't there.

Heather cupped her hands around her mouth. "Rocket! Here, boy!"

Nothing.

I scanned the yard, my heart sinking.

Rocket was gone.

"Brooke?" Heather put a hand on my shoulder. "I don't think Rocket's in the yard anymore."

"Did he sneak past us and go inside?" I dashed back into the house, running from room to room, stopping in the kitchen and calling his name. Even if he was trapped somewhere, he could at least bark, but the only sound was

Heather's footsteps behind mine.

"I'm going to call Tim and Vanessa and see if they can help," she said, pulling out her cell phone.

I stopped her. "No, it's fine. I can handle this."

Heather started texting anyway. "With four of us, we can search faster."

"I've got this, really," I said, reaching for her cell phone.

She twisted away. "Then they can help with your advice letters while—"

"STOP!" I finally shouted.

"WHY?" Heather replied.

I stepped back, startled. Heather doesn't get loud. And Heather doesn't scowl. But she was doing both of those at the moment.

"Brooke, what is going on with you? Why won't you let your friends help? It's not like we're trying to steal credit." She flopped down onto a kitchen chair. "And to be honest, it's a little insulting. Like you don't think we're capable of doing anything."

I sighed and sat across from her. "It's not you guys; it's me. I'm the one who's incapable: of writing a script, of keeping up with the advice column . . . and every time someone has to help, it just proves even more that I'm not cut out to do anything." I traced the patterns on a placemat.

"Brooke, that's ridiculous," said Heather.

"Is it?" I asked. "Last year, I did soccer, coed baseball, made honor roll, and still had time for my family and friends. This year, I'm failing at every-thing." I got up and opened the cabinet under the kitchen sink, pulling out a flashlight. I flicked it on and off to test it. "But I'm not going to fail at this."

"What are you doing?" asked Heather, join-ing me.

"It'll be dark soon. I'm going to look for Rocket." I paused. "Will you please stay here in case he comes back, and call me if he does?"

Heather's forehead wrinkled, but she nodded. "Of course."

I sprinted out the front door and took a right down the street, softly calling Rocket's name. I wandered the neighborhood until the sun went down. Then I flicked on the flashlight and retraced my steps.

At the end of the street was a park, the only other place Rocket would go, but between the street and the park was a busy intersection. If Rocket had tried to gallop across that with his usual carefree style, he wouldn't be paying attention to the rush of cars.

"Rocket!" I now shouted.

I paused at the street corner to wait for traffic to pass, glancing in both directions, hoping and praying I didn't see any furry lumps in the road. When there was a small break in the cars, I dashed across all four lanes and almost collided with the park fence.

Closed after dark.

"Crud!"

The fence bars were too narrow for me to squeeze through, but I could climb over if I had something to get me started. A nearby trash can was the perfect boost, and I was over the fence in just a few minutes.

"Rocket!" I whispered, in case there might be park security.

A rustling of leaves from a nearby bush made me jump. But then I heard a panting sound.

"Rocket! Come on, boy!" I got down on my knees and clapped my hands. "Want a tummy rub?"

More panting, and a snout poked through the bushes.

It was not Rocket's. It was way too big to be Rocket's.

And there would be no tummy rub.

I lowered the flashlight. The snout pushed

forward, sniffing the air. I remained in my crouch but backed up several paces. My sneakers shuffled in the dirt, and the dog growled, revealing its massive head, along with several teeth capable of ripping a sixth grader into kibble-sized bites.

"Good dog," I said. "Nice dog. Vegan dog?"

The dog barked and lunged forward, but the branches of the bush caught it. It struggled to reach me, snapping branches and shaking leaves on to the ground. I screamed and scrambled to my feet, running back toward the fence. The beast lunging after me barked with wild abandon, each bark sounding closer than the last.

"Please, oh, please!" I said to nobody in particular. "I don't want to die!"

I broke the tree line and was almost to the fence when I saw Vanessa, Heather, and Tim on the other side.

"Back up, back up!" I shouted.

"Brooke! How did you get over there?" asked Heather.

"Believe me, you don't want to be on this side!" I grabbed the top of the fence and tried to scale it, but it was too tall without something to boost me.

Vanessa was apparently thinking the same thing. "Heather, help me," she said, getting down on one knee and reaching through the fence. Heather imitated her pose, and they clasped their palms together.

Just as I stepped into their hands, the dog shot through the trees, barking and snarling. Heather and Vanessa screamed and let me go, clutching each other.

"Hey!" Tim flicked pebbles through the fence toward the dog. "Over here!"

It faltered for a second, startled by the presence of so many humans.

In that brief hesitation something even wilder

happened. Tires screeched, and a horn blared directly to my right as the front of a car stopped inches from the fence.

"Get out of here, you mongrel!" shouted the driver.

My eyes went wide and tearful. "Dad!"

"Are you okay, honey?"

Of course I was. My *dad* was here.

"I'm fine!" I turned back to face the dog, a little bit braver. "Get out of here!" I picked up my own handful of pebbles and flung them.

Screaming people, blinding headlights, and flying objects were finally too much for the dog. It growled and disappeared back into the bushes. As soon as it did, I whirled to face my friends.

"Now get *me* out of here!"

Heather and Vanessa both crouched by the fence again, and this time I pulled myself up and over. Dad waited to grab me, arms uplifted.

"What on *Earth* were you doing in there?"

he asked, hugging me close while I cried into his shoulder.

"Rocket ran away!" I sobbed.

"And you thought you'd ask that nice dog if it'd seen him?" asked Dad.

I know he was trying to make me feel better, but I couldn't laugh.

"Rocket's probably dead somewhere, and it's all my fault!" I wailed.

"Oh, I doubt that," said Dad. "Rocket's pretty smart. I think Miss Lillian told me he used to run obstacle courses."

"We'll help you find him," Tim told me.

I should've been grateful, but instead I just cried even harder.

"Is she . . . is she deeply moved by my gesture?" Tim asked my dad.

"Dumb, old, incompetent Brooke can't do anything. She always needs help," I blubbered into Dad's shoulder.

"What?" he said, leaning back to look at me.

"Brooke, that's not what Tim's saying," said Vanessa, putting a hand on my back.

"I think you're being a little hard on yourself," agreed Heather. "You say you're incompetent and that you can't do anything."

I motioned for Dad to put me down.

"It's true," I said.

"No," said Heather. "Brooke, it's not that you can't do anything. It's that you can't do *everything*. Not unless you have a dozen clones running around."

"But I *should* be able to," I said. "My dad does." I looked up at him.

Dad dropped down to one knee. "You think I don't pay for it? I work more than I sleep, and I miss spending time with you and your mom."

"And *you* have zero time for a personal life too," Vanessa told me. "That's why you're struggling to balance it all. You're trying to keep everyone happy."

"I had the perfect plan," I said. "I was going to dominate this year." I pounded a fist into my palm. "Do everything, win everything . . ."

"And give everything one hundred percent, which is great," said Heather. "But when you're stretched so thin, you're only giving a fraction of yourself to each thing."

"We miss having *all* of our Brooke," said Vanessa.

"I'll bet even your secret admirer feels neglected," Tim teased.

My friends laughed and I smiled.

"Secret admirer?" Dad raised an eyebrow.

I wrapped my arm through his. "Just this guy who leaves me notes like 'You're okay to look at' and 'You're different.'"

"Charming," said Dad.

Heather bumped me. "You didn't tell him that each one is sealed with a heart."

There was that strange tingling feeling again; this time, stronger.

"Yeah," I said, wrinkling my forehead.

"Anyway, we just want you to be happy," said Vanessa, giving me a squeeze. "We love you."

"We love you sooo much," said Heather.

"I think you're just okay," said Tim.

"And your mother and I love you too. Don't take life so seriously," said Dad, giving me a smile. "You have to enjoy it."

I hugged him and gave my friends a group squeeze. "You guys are the best."

Dad glanced at his watch. "And now I think it's time to resume the search for old Rocket."

"Actually"—I tugged on Dad's sleeve—"I think I know where he might be."

"Okay," he said, herding us all toward the car. "Where to?"

"Let's return to the scene of the crime," I said.

"The scene of the crime, Officer?" Tim repeated with a snort.

"Young Sherlock," I corrected him. At the amused looks from Heather and Vanessa, I added, "I've got to start somewhere, and the Hound of the Berryville is as good a place as any."

"You made a humorous play off a book title!" Tim clapped a hand over his heart. "I'm so proud."

Dad chuckled and backed the car on to the street. "Miss Lillian's, it is."

As he drove I explained my thought process to my friends.

"Rocket used to run obstacle courses, which means he's talented at navigating more than a straight path on the ground. He can run around things, up things, over things, and through things."

"So he's running through all the fences in the neighborhood, leaving Rocket-shaped holes?" asked Tim.

I laughed along with everyone else. "Not through fences, *up* fences. Fence boards, to be exact."

"No of*fense*," said Vanessa, smirking at her own pun, "but that would mean climbing vertically, and no dog is that talented."

"He could climb a fence board if . . ." I looked to Heather, who clapped a hand to her forehead.

"If it was angled against something. The shelter!"

"The shelter?" Dad repeated, applying the brakes. "Am I going to the animal shelter now?"

"No, Dad," I said. "Keep driving. See, I built a pretend shelter for my history video, leaning old boards against Miss Lillian's shed. After some of them fell on Heather, I took her inside to get first aid."

Vanessa clutched Heather's arm. "Oh my gosh! Are you okay?"

"It's bad. The doctors say I only have eighty

more years to live," Heather replied with a wink. Vanessa pushed her.

"Anyway," I said, "some of the boards fell because Rocket ran into them when he got excited over a ham bone I was carrying. When Heather got hurt, I threw the ham bone into the grass because her life is more important than old pork."

"Thank you," said Heather.

Dad pulled the car into Miss Lillian's driveway, and I said a quick prayer of thanks that she hadn't come home yet. Everyone got out, and my friends and Dad followed me into the backyard.

"That's where I dropped the bone," I said, pointing to the grass. "Notice anything?"

"There's no bone," said Vanessa.

"So Rocket took it when you were inside," said Tim. "Then he walked up the boards leaning against the shed and . . ."

We all moved in a cluster toward the shed,

and I shone my flashlight on the boards propped against it, the tops of which ended just below a broken section of the shed's window.

"No way," said Dad.

I crept up to the shed and shone my light inside.

There was Rocket, snoring on his stomach, bone nestled between his front paws.

"Mystery solved," I said with a smile.

Dad clapped a hand on my shoulder and grinned. "We'll let Miss Lillian get him out later. Everyone back in the house."

"I don't understand," said Heather. "Why didn't he bark when we were calling his name?"

"If you'd just sneaked off with a treat, would you want someone to find you and take it away?" I asked.

"Good point," she said. "So now what? The star of your film is napping in his trailer, so to speak."

"Yes, but I have . . . human stars?" I looked hopefully at my friends. "Please? It'll only take, like, thirty minutes."

"Is Brooke Jacobs asking for help?" Vanessa gasped. "How can this be?"

Heather put a finger to her lips. "Shhh! She might change her mind. Be cool!"

"Oh, you guys are a riot," I said, rolling my eyes. I turned to Dad. "Do you think it's okay if we use Miss Lillian's yard?"

"I don't see why not," he said with a shrug. "I'll sit out here with you, just in case, though. Let me tell Mom." He stepped into the house to make a call.

"He does realize you guys live right across the street, doesn't he?" said Tim. "He could just walk over there and come back later to check on us."

I watched my dad through the window. "I don't mind if he stays here."

I didn't mind one bit.

Even with a ready-made script and Dad's help directing, I knew the video wasn't going to turn out as good as the original, but it made me feel better to know that at least I'd tried. Plus, Miss Lillian gave us all desserts when she came back from her meeting. She didn't even mind freeing Rocket from the shed. In fact, she seemed a little proud.

"I guess an old dog can teach himself new tricks," she said with a chuckle.

Dad offered to drive all my friends home, and I insisted they go, even after Heather offered to stay the night to help me catch up on everything.

Before she got into the car, she turned to me. "You know I love you, right?"

"Yes, and I'm sorry for how I acted earlier."

We hugged, and she held on to my arms for an extra minute. "Something's gotta give, Brooke, or you're going to implode."

I nodded. As much as I hated to admit it, she was right.

When I got back to my house, I added narration to the history video we'd made (correctly this time) and studied for a science quiz that I was fairly certain I was going to fail. After that I tackled my three questions for the website and was just about to work on the Young Sherlocks mystery when Mom insisted I go to sleep.

The next morning I dragged myself out of bed half an hour early, got dressed, and grabbed a blueberry muffin before heading out the front door.

"Bye," I told my parents. "It's going to be a long day at the office."

"Well, thank goodness it's Friday!" Mom chirped after me.

Normally, I would've agreed, but I couldn't celebrate today . . . not with the task I had ahead of me.

With every step closer to school, my heart beat a little faster. The lights were on in the Journalism room, and the door was open, so I took a deep breath and walked inside.

"Mrs. H . . ."

But the only person in the room was Mary Patrick, flipping through a dictionary with a pencil between her teeth and the table in front of her covered with papers.

We both froze at the sight of each other.

"What are you doing here? Is it after noon already?" asked Mary Patrick. She glanced at the clock.

"I need to talk to Mrs. H," I said.

"She's going to be absent today," said Mary Patrick. "As is our copy editor, which means I have to copyedit twenty pages myself, and I'm fairly certain *radicchio* isn't a real word." She slammed the dictionary shut and pushed it off the table.

"Oh," I said. "Well, I guess I can just tell you."

Mary Patrick sifted through some papers. "You're not here to gloat about the success of your column, are you? Because if you are, I'm going to need some chocolate."

"No, actually." I twisted my fingers together and cleared my throat. "I'm quitting the paper."

Plan B(rooke)

Mary Patrick reached up and smacked herself across the face. "Ow."

I backed up. "Whoa!"

I wasn't sure what kind of reaction to expect, but it definitely wasn't *that*.

"Just checking to see if I'm awake," she said. "At first I thought I was dreaming because I'd love to see the advice column dissolve into nothingness, but you're still here, and a giant chocolate bar *isn't*, so clearly I'm having a nightmare." She rubbed her cheek. "A very painful one."

"Well, the column isn't going away," I said. "Just me."

She put down the pages she was looking at. "Can I ask why?"

"Because . . . I'm no good," I said, my voice suddenly shaky. "You want a perfect paper, and I'm only going to ruin it." I flopped down in a chair beside her.

She frowned. "What's going on? I don't like this. I'm feeling a strange urge to hug you and tell you everything will be okay."

"But it won't," I said. "Not as long as I'm on the paper. I'm screwing up everything I touch, and I can't seem to get anything done."

Mary Patrick gave me a withering look. "You realize it's only the second week of school," she said. "And you're only a sixth grader. I highly doubt you've inflicted that much damage." She turned in her chair to face me. "Explain."

And so I told her about everything that had happened so far: soccer, student council, Young Sherlocks, my history project, Gabby's dating fiasco, the advice column, Rocket . . .

She whistled through her teeth.

"You really keep busy, Jacobs! And I think that's a big part of your problem."

"That's what everyone says." I rested my chin on my hand. "Except I *like* being busy."

Mary Patrick nodded. "I'm exactly the same way. But let me show you something."

She got up and walked to the far wall, which was lined with bookshelves containing yearbooks from the past twenty years. She selected one toward the end and flipped through it, holding it out for my inspection.

"This is my sixth-grade picture." She pointed to a black box with "No photo available" stamped on it and her name printed underneath. "I missed picture day and picture retake day. In fact, I missed a whole month of school and had to make it up during the summer."

"What happened to you?" I asked, giving her a quick once-over. "And is it contagious?"

"You seem to have caught it, so yes," she said, closing the yearbook. "It's called 'burnout'— when you push yourself so hard you get mentally, physically, and emotionally exhausted. And it'll happen to you if you don't use your time more wisely and say . . . 'TADA!'" She approached the dry-erase board.

"'Ta-da'?" I repeated.

"TADA is the Mary Patrick productivity model." She started writing on the board:

Take notes
Analyze
Decide
Act

She faced me and frowned. "Why aren't you writing this down? 'Take notes' is the first step of TADA." She gestured to the board.

"Sorry," I said, getting out a notebook and searching for a clean sheet. I flipped past the start of my letter to Overwhelmed and Miserable, and inspiration hit me. "Would you mind if I included your tips in my advice column?"

"Really?" Mary Patrick blushed and started to smile but then remembered the fierce editor that she was. "Wait, so you're going to stay with the paper?"

I nodded. "I really like it here. I'll just have to sacrifice something else."

"All right, then," said Mary Patrick. "Let's go over the second part of TADA: analyzing. Is this task a good use of my time?"

She talked until the bell rang for homeroom, but I had more than enough info to help Overwhelmed and Miserable *and* to get everything in order in my world.

As I left the newsroom, I pulled all the advice requests out of the box. When I got to home-room, I sorted through them with Vanessa's help, jotting down all the ones with school-related complaints. Then I went to the library and researched the different uses for citrus fruit.

At lunch I laced up my cleats and got ready to run some soccer plays, but when I stepped out-side, I wasn't alone. My dad was waiting for me.

"What are *you* doing here?" I tackled him with a hug.

"I thought you could use someone to play off of," he said, hiking his athletic shorts to Embarrassing Dad level. "And I realize if I want you to listen to my advice, I should probably practice what I preach."

For an entire glorious hour, I had my dad to myself, doing what I loved most. And at the start of history class, I told my teacher the truth: that the other members of my team had done a great job and how I'd messed up the project all on my own.

When my history group sat down, they were eager to watch the video.

"Don't be," I said. "I have a confession to make. I accidentally deleted the video. And I am so sorry!"

Three horrified gasps from three devastated faces.

"But some friends and I refilmed it," I added.

"And it's even better?" asked Gabby with a hopeful smile.

"No, it's far worse," I said. "*But* the good news is that Mr. Costas is going to let the three of you redo the video, and I will help with whatever you need."

"What about you?" asked Ashley.

"I'm getting a fifty," I said, "and grounded as soon as my parents find out. But it'll be nice to spend some time at home." I gave them all a tight smile. "Again, I'm really sorry."

Spencer nodded. "It's cool. Plus, now I can add some more stuff to the video that I forgot the first time."

Gabby prodded me. "You said the good news was that we got to remake the video. What was the bad news?"

I pointed to the front of the class. "Mr. Costas still wants to air the video that Tim, Heather, Vanessa, and I made."

Someone turned off the lights, and the video opened with my friends and me in Miss Lillian's backyard, scooping stew out of a bowl with our bare hands.

"I can't wait until spoons are invented," whispered Mesopotamian Tim.

Offscreen, Miss Lillian's porch light flickered. Heather squealed in mock fright. "The moon is going out!"

Several people laughed, including me. Across

the classroom, I could see Heather with her hands over her face, but she was smiling. When the video ended, everyone applauded and cheered.

"What did we learn from this film?" asked Mr. Costas.

"That Tim Antonides invented spoons!" someone shouted.

"What did we learn about ancient society?" amended Mr. Costas. "Did the Mesopotamians live alone?"

A guy raised his hand. "No, they lived in family units, just like we do."

Mr. Costas nodded. "Why?"

The class talked about early family life, and then we watched and laughed at more videos until the end of class. When Spencer got up to go, I tapped his shoulder.

"I have something for you," I said, handing him a folded piece of paper.

He opened it.

"It's for your student council platform," I told him. "A list of the things kids want fixed in this school. I thought you could maybe make some changes in the government."

His lips moved as he read, broadening into a wide smile. "These are awesome! Why aren't you using them?"

I shook my head. "I'm not going to run for office. I thought it would be fun to be in a position of power, but after *really* thinking about it, it's not for me."

"Well . . . thanks!" Spencer said, saluting me with the paper and slipping it into his notebook. "I'll definitely use these."

"Good luck!" I told him.

"Hey!" Heather bumped me. "I can't believe how horrible we were in that video!" She giggled.

I gave her a look of mock disappointment. "You don't think we'll be winning any awards?"

We walked together out of the classroom.

"Are you going to be able to join us for Musketeer Movies tomorrow?" she asked.

"I think I could find the time," I said.

I turned to the right, to go down the main hallway, instead of turning to left, and Heather grabbed my arm.

"Wrong way, lady."

"Nope," I said. "There's one more person I have to talk to. I'll catch up with you later."

I took a deep breath and entered the seventh-grade hall, *very* aware of all eyes on me, a lowly sixth grader in the wrong neck of the woods. But I knew exactly where I was going.

The guy that I was looking for was at the water fountain by the seventh-grade bathrooms, and when he saw me, he straightened up and smirked.

"Abel Fenimore Hart." I handed him a print-out with the information I'd been granted after correctly solving the Young Sherlocks' puzzle.

Abel's middle name: Fenimore

"Looks like you took my advice and did some research," said Abel.

I nodded. "Orange juice makes a great invisible ink, but you don't really need the peel, do you? You hold the inked document up to a heat source, and you can read the writing. And once you're done writing the note, you can eat the fruit."

"And it was delicious." He patted his stomach. "Welcome to the club."

"Thanks," I said. "And here's something for you." I handed him an envelope decorated with heart-shaped stickers.

"What's all this?" he asked with a grin.

"Isn't that how you identify yourself, Mr. Hart?" I pulled out one of the notes from my secret admirer, pointing to the heart.

I could see dimples in his cheeks now. "Took you long enough to figure it out."

"I wasn't sure I wanted to," I said. "What if

my secret admirer had turned out to be a major disappointment?"

"Some risks are just worth taking," he said, blushing. "Right?"

I studied him for a moment and then smiled. "Only time will tell."

"Speaking of risks . . ." He held the envelope up to the light. "I'm afraid to ask what's in here."

"It's a gift certificate to Giordano's Pizza." It was my turn to blush. "You may have been right about some things, and your help came in handy. So thanks."

Abel shook his head, opening the envelope. "I can't eat a whole pizza by myself," he said, studying the certificate. "And I know you've missed out at lunch since you've been playing soccer by yourself. Sad, by the way."

He dodged a punch that I threw at him.

"How about you redeem this with me?" He waved the certificate.

My eyes lit up. "Really? I love pizza!"

"I know," he said, smiling.

"It's a deal!" I said. "So when is the first meeting of Young Sherlocks?"

"Next Wednesday," he said. "Can you make it?"

"Absolutely," I said as the warning bell rang. "Later!"

I ran to my last class, but it felt more like I was flying. All my worries and weights had been lifted off my shoulders. I aced my quiz and spent the rest of class writing my letter to Overwhelmed and Miserable.

When the bell rang, I dashed to the newsroom with the hard copy, but Mary Patrick was out, so I handed it to Stefan.

"Hi, I already emailed the copy but could you please make sure she gets this too? Thanks, and have a good weekend!" I breezed out of the room.

"Uh. Sure!" he called. "You too!"

I knew that I would.

Saturday's Musketeer Movies actually turned out to include a special guest, with Tim sprawled on one of the couches.

"I hope you don't mind that I invited him," said Heather, pulling me aside. "I just figured he's one of us now."

"One of the girls? I'm sure he'd be pleased to know that."

She laughed. "So do you feel better now that you're all caught up?"

We joined Vanessa and Tim in the living room.

"I do," I said, "but I'm wondering what's going to happen next."

"What do you mean?" asked Vanessa.

"Well, we just started middle school," I said. "If all this happened in just a few weeks, who knows what's around the corner?"

"Ahh, we can take it, whatever it is," said Tim, waving a dismissive hand.

"I agree," said Heather, pouring soda into four glasses. "A toast to us! And whatever lies ahead!"

We all picked up a glass.

"To us!" we cheered.

"And to Brooke!" crowed Vanessa. "Newest team captain for the Berryville Strikers!"

I grinned so broadly my cheeks hurt.

Coach had started Saturday's practice with that announcement, praising my willingness to follow orders, my winning attitude, and my ability to be a team player. Lacey had turned a furious purple with absolutely no help from snow-cone syrup.

"To Brooke!" Vanessa, Heather, and Tim cheered at the same time I roared, "To me!"

"And to me!" said Tim.

We regarded him curiously.

"In addition to the advice column, you're

looking at the backup sportswriter." He preened and flexed his muscles.

"What?"

"No way!"

"How?" I asked. "I thought Stefan refused to budge."

He shrugged. "Apparently, he's got a lot on his plate with swimming and photography and trying to get into this exclusive high school next year. He told me he was overwhelmed and miserable."

I almost choked on my soda.

Vanessa patted my back. "You okay?"

"Fine," I managed with a cough. "Wrong pipe."

"*Anyway*," said Tim, "he asked me to help out."

"Woo-hoo!" said Vanessa. "To Tim!"

"To Tim!" we all cheered.

"And to pizza!" said Heather, holding a box out to me. "I know you can never get enough."

I laughed. "*Everybody* knows. Abel Hart even invited me to have half his pizza when he goes."

"What?!"

"No way!"

"I'm feeling déjà vu," said Tim.

Vanessa pawed at my shoulder. "You're going on a date with Abel?"

I gave her a strange look. "No. I gave him a gift certificate to Giordano's, and he asked me to redeem it with him, and oh my God, I'm going on a date with Abel." I buried my face in my hands.

Tim patted my leg. "Excellent sleuthing, detective."

Heather and Vanessa burst out laughing until I hit them both with a pillow. This launched a full-scale retaliation of flying feathers, which turned into an assault of flying pizza. Pepperoni, of course. Because I've got the best friends in the world.

Dear Overwhelmed and Miserable,

I can totally relate to your situation, and here's my advice: rank everything you have to do by importance, then tackle the important stuff first. Take notes so you don't forget anything. Don't accept more than you can handle, be realistic about your deadlines, and above all, don't be afraid to ask for help! Even Babe Ruth went to his coach for advice every once in a while.

Confidentially yours,
Brooke Jacobs

Acknowledgments

Always for family, friends, and God.

For Andrea Martin, who put faith in my funny.

For Annie Berger, who knows how to make my stories better.

For Jenn Laughran, who's always in my corner.

For Martha Flynn and Whitney Miller, who don't bat an eye when I need a spontaneous trip to San Francisco.

For Mari Mancusi, my goals pal, who keeps me on track and brainstorms with me, whether it's about the book world or the real world.

For Cory Oakes, who has one of the sweetest hearts and will be reincarnated as a unicorn.

For Michael Reisman, who is one of the most patient and hilarious people I know.

For Cindy Pon and her Sweet Pea, who are such wonderful cheerleaders of my work.

For the Slaughters, who help me have a life outside the book world.

And for Cecille Neuman and Amanda Pisana, who I can be silly and serious with and who never judge my cartwheels.

Turn the page for a sneak peek at the next
book in the *Confidentially Yours* series:

VANESSA'S FASHION FACE-OFF

CHAPTER

1

Fashion Passion

This was the night I'd been waiting for.

With one hand I pulled back a glossy blue curtain and squinted against the stage lights for a glimpse at the audience—A-list celebs chatted on folding chairs, Badgley Mischka and Birkin bags tucked under their seats. Some of them saw me and whispered excitedly, waving and snapping photos with their phones.

I grinned and humored them with a pose before retreating backstage. No time to flaunt; I had models to prep for the runway.

The models gathered for inspection, each

wearing a piece from my new fall line. I paused in front of one and adjusted her shoulder strap for a better silhouette.

Glancing at my watch, I ushered the models to follow the choreographer and readied myself at the side of the stage.

The master of ceremonies winked at me, raised his microphone, and said, "Little girl, can you ask your brother to stop licking the window?"

"Huh?"

I blinked, and the runway disappeared, replaced by a ball gown–wearing mannequin in a store window display. And I wasn't backstage in Paris. I was on the sidewalk in Chicago, glancing up at a man in a sharp black suit accessorized with . . . a security badge.

"I said, can you get your brother to stop licking the window?" he asked. "I'm assuming he is your brother."

He pointed to a young boy standing inside the display, tongue pressed to the glass like a dog slobbering on a porch screen.

My first impulse was to say, "No, sir, I do *not* know that kid waving at us!" and run through traffic to escape.

But since my brother, Terrell, and I look so much alike—same dimples, same wild Afros, same gold-flecked eyes—there was nothing I could do but sigh.

"Yes, sir. I'll get him."

I turned to go inside and then stopped in front of the revolving entry door.

"Well?" pressed the security guard.

"Uh . . . I'm not . . ."

I wasn't sure how to finish. He wouldn't believe me if I told him revolving doors were my enemies. Actually, doors in general were my enemies. And corners of furniture. And gravity.

I'm kind of clumsy.

"Never mind," I said. "Wish me luck."

Sure enough, as the door went around, I misjudged the opening and barely squeezed through in time, losing a shoe in the process.

"Crud." I hopped on one foot, waiting for an opening, and then leaping into the space between two panels just as the security guard went around the other side, holding my shoe. "Double crud!"

I was so glad nobody from Abraham Lincoln Middle School could see this, especially my teammates at "Lincoln's Letters," our school newspaper's advice column. Besides working together, those three were also my best friends, and I knew exactly how they'd react.

Brooke Jacobs, our tomboy with fiery-red hair, would've injected some sort of sports commentary.

Heather Schwartz—our adorable, gap-toothed songbird—would've said, "Oh, sweetie!"

and taken off one of her shoes so I wouldn't feel so bad.

And Tim Antonides—our tall, dark-haired comedian—would've joked, "The revolving door god is pleased with your offering."

Since they weren't around, I quietly accepted my shoe from the security guard, slipped it on, and went inside. Terrell giggled when he saw me and sprinted behind a clothes rack.

"Terrell!" I whispered as loud as I dared. "Get back here or I won't play Battle the Mermaid with you anymore!"

It was a game my brother came up with that's basically hide-and-seek with his special treasures. I, the mermaid, steal them, and he has to get them back. Since I'm allowed to dress up, I don't complain about playing.

My brother scampered over, and I scooted him toward the door, holding the belt loop at the back of his jeans.

"Why were you licking the window?" I asked.

"I wasn't licking the window!" He shot me an offended look. "I was making a tongue print."

I busted out laughing. I couldn't help it.

If someone asked my friends to describe me, they'd probably say I was overly cheerful and positive, especially given the number of ridiculous things that happen to me on a daily basis. I don't think that's a bad thing. It's better than being the girl who cries if she spills something on her favorite top.

Don't get me wrong; fashion disasters aren't to be taken lightly, but you can either sulk or solve the problem. And I always choose to set things right.

I nodded to the security guard, who stood in front of the revolving door and gestured to one side.

A regular door next to the revolving one. Imagine.

I smiled at him. "Now we're talking!"

My brother, who had no idea what was going on, ignored both of us and pushed through the door to step outside.

Our car was already there, and Mom was leaning across to shout out the passenger window.

"Come on, you two! I'm blocking traffic!"

Terrell and I ran over, me hopping into the front seat and him in the back.

"I'm sorry that took so long," said Mom. "Getting out of the garage was a nightmare."

"It's Michigan Ave.," I told her. "If there's no traffic, it's the apocalypse."

Michigan Avenue, aka the Magnificent Mile, was famous for its stores, restaurants, and hotels. Normally, Mom wouldn't leave Berryville, the nearby suburb where we live, to venture out among the hundreds of tourists and shoppers, but she'd wanted to visit my grandma at her retirement home in the city. And while we were there, Grandma had given me something extra special for my Halloween costume.

For someone who loves fashion as much as I do, Halloween is like Christmas and my birthday rolled into one. A chance to dress up and get rewarded for it with candy. But this year the candy wasn't even the big draw. This year it was the Schwartzes' Halloween party. For the first time, Heather, Brooke, Tim, and I would be old enough to attend, and if the stories Heather's older brothers told were true, the party would be epic.

I'd been working on my costume since midsummer, and with a week to go, it was almost done. I'd just needed one last piece, which I'd picked up today at Grandma's: a Victorian cameo brooch with the carving of a young woman's face in it. Grandma made me swear up and down that I wouldn't lose it and that I'd go to church with her because she loves going and wearing fancy hats. (I guess my fashion bug had to come from somewhere.)

By the time we got home, it was dark, and Terrell was passed out cold in the backseat. Mom hoisted him over one shoulder.

"Could you bring in the bags, please?" She popped the trunk and moved some For Sale signs that had fallen on them.

Mom's a Realtor, which I love because she gets to "dress" homes to show off to potential buyers *and* she bakes cookies that Terrell and I get to sample before open houses. People weren't sure she could make it on her own after my dad passed away, and that was before Terrell was even born. But my mom showed the world how strong a woman can be, and she's one of the main reasons I want to make a name for myself. Like mother, like daughter!

Mom carried Terrell inside, and I grabbed

the bags, clutching hers in one hand and my four in the other, wishing I'd put on my gloves. It was only October, but the nights were already getting chilly. Still, I loved how it added to the spookiness of the season.

I closed the trunk and turned around.

A pale face popped up in front of mine.

"Hey!" it said.

"Augh! Child ghost!" I flailed my arms, shopping bags whipping back and forth. One of the bags struck the ghost squarely in the shoulder.

"Ow!"

Whoops. Solid body? Not a ghost.

"Sorry!" I said, lowering the bags.

"Oh gosh, no, *I'm* sorry!" The mystery girl rubbed her arm. "In my head, that was supposed to end more delightfully."

"Are you okay?" I asked.

She rotated her shoulder. "I think so. Luckily, I only use this arm for holding purses."

I wasn't sure if she was joking, so I glanced up and down the street. "Where did you come from?"

"Los Angeles," she said.

I laughed. "No, I meant just now."

"Oh!" She laughed too. "My folks and I just moved in across the street."

She pointed to a blue two-story with an SUV in the driveway.

"You came from California with all your stuff in that?" I asked.

She made a face. And then an entire road trip's worth of conversation came out.

"Actually, a moving van was with us, but it broke down, steaming, smoking . . . the works!" She threw her hands in the air for emphasis. "So it's still a day behind. We packed some extra clothes in the car because you never know what state calls for what outfit; like, for California, you need a sweater, but in Arizona you don't, but in Colorado you do! So we didn't have any room for dishware, and my parents are supereco and don't believe in plastic forks, so they wanted me to ask if you had three regular ones we could borrow."

I blinked as my brain caught up with her words. "Three . . . forks?"

She nodded. "Nonplastic, please."

"Uh . . . sure! Follow me," I said, adjusting my bags. "I'm Vanessa, by the way."

"Katie," she said. "Here, let me help." She eyed the label on one of the bags she grabbed. "You went shopping at Fitzhugh's? I love that store!"

"Me too!" I said. "They have the best leggings."

"The best," she agreed. Then she gasped and held up another bag. "And you went to Barneys? You must be swimming in the green. Is your pool filled with twenties?"

I laughed again. "No, I buy stuff on sale and

then rework it into something better. Fashion is kind of my passion."

Katie squealed and threw her arms around me. "Mine too!" She immediately stepped back. "Sorry! That was weird since we haven't even exchanged forks. But I'm so happy to meet someone my age—at least, I'm assuming you're my age?"

"I'm twelve," I said.

"Me too!" She bounced up and down. "And I'm also assuming you probably hate polyester?"

"It's the worst!" I said, and we both laughed.

The front door opened and Mom poked her head out. "Vanessa?" She spotted Katie and opened the door wider. "Well, hello there!"

"Mom, this is Katie," I said, nudging my new friend closer to the door. "She and her folks moved in across the street, but their stuff hasn't gotten here yet. Can they borrow some forks?"

"I think we can do a little better than that,"

said Mom with a wink. "Come inside, girls."

Katie and I followed Mom into the kitchen.

Now that there was more light, I could see that Katie was definitely a girl after my own heart. She was wearing black satiny harem pants with a white crop top. Although I personally would've added a blue scarf to bring out the color of her eyes.

Mom grabbed a basket from the pantry and set it on the counter. "Give me a second to put together a little something for your parents," she said to Katie.

Katie nodded. "Thank you, Ms. . . ."

"Jackson," I supplied. "Can you hand me those bags?" I nodded to the ones Katie was holding. "Unless you want to follow me to my room."

Katie nodded again, still wide-eyed. "I'd love to see your reworked clothes."

I stared at her, awestruck. "Really?"

This was a designer's dream: a request to see their work. Mind you, the requestor was a twelve-year-old girl who wasn't going to carry my label and make me rich, but I'd take what I could get.

"Can I show Katie my stuff?" I asked Mom.

She smiled. "I'll holler for you when I'm done here."

Katie followed me down the hall, and when I flipped on the light to my room, she gasped and ran up to one of my walls. "I love this!"

The whole wall was nothing but cork, so it looked like a giant bulletin board. I'd pinned magazine pages and sketches I'd drawn on one half, and tacked up photos of family and friends on the other.

"The real wall is still behind it," I said. "This is just paneling."

"And who are these girls?" She pointed to one of many photos of Brooke, Heather, and me.

"Those are my best friends from school," I said. "We write an advice column for our school paper, the *Lincoln Log*. Brooke writes about sports and fitness"—I pointed to her—"and Heather writes about relationships and friendships." I pointed her out in a different picture, along with Tim. "And Tim writes the guy's perspective."

"And you write about fashion?" asked Katie. "Brilliant idea to showcase your talent!"

"Well, Brooke gets the credit," I said. "The newspaper needed some space filled, and she suggested it. She's always excited to try new things."

I left out the part where Brooke's overeagerness had overwhelmed her in the first month of school and that we were lucky to even still have her on the paper.

"But I bet you're the best columnist," said Katie. "Or at least . . . the best dressed!"

"But of course!" I presented one of my tops with a flourish.

Katie oohed and aahed appropriately, inspecting the stitching. "This is so professional! You have got to be the coolest person I've ever met, Vanessa."

I beamed. "Thanks. I put a lot of blood, sweat, and tears into each piece."

That wasn't just a figure of speech, either. Learning to use a needle was a painful process.

Katie toyed with the sleeve of one of the tops and asked, almost bashfully, "Want to see some of my work?"

I wrinkled my forehead. "I thought your moving van—"

"No, on my website. Do you have a computer I can use?"

"You have a website?" I asked, reaching for my laptop. "Aren't you afraid someone's going to steal your designs?"

She shook her head. "The website's public, but my portfolio is in a private section, so only I can access it, but I can share it with people if they sign a privacy agreement."

Katie took the laptop from me and started typing.

"Have you actually needed to make people sign the agreement?" I dared to ask.

She shrugged. "A couple magazines that wanted to interview me."

"A couple . . . Interview?" The words barely made it past my lips.

Katie turned my laptop so I could see the page. "Here we go!"

My mind . . . was blown.

This was the kind of website I dreamed of having in ten years, and Katie had it now. Adorable pop music in the background, a video of her giving fashion tips, links for interviews and podcasts she'd done . . .

In the center of it all was a dress rack that you could hover over to pull out one of her designs and look at. And her designs were good. I had half a mind to take back the top I'd shown her and say, "Kidding! My six-year-old brother made these."

"What do you think?" she asked shyly.

"I think," I said with a nervous smile, "that this town just got a little more interesting."

EXTRA, EXTRA!
READ ALL ABOUT BROOKE, TIM, VANESSA, & HEATHER IN THE

Confidentially YOURS
SERIES!